ISHANA

A GIRL IN MY DREAMS

DURGADAS BR

First Published 2021

BecomeShakespeare.com

One Point Six Technologies Pvt Ltd
123, Building J2, Shram Seva Premises,
Wadala Truck Depot, Wadala (East),
Mumbai 400037, India
T: +91 8080226699

ISBN - 978-93-5438-705-0

Dedicated to:

YOU

Contents

Introduction 9

Prologue 13

Prajwal 17

My First Insult 21

My Dream Girl 27

New Beginnings 33

Time 49

Royal Mech 53

My Attitude 57

Just Part Of Destiny 65

Facebook 73

B For Boxing 81

Gay-Dian Angel 89

Spy Report 99

The First And Last 105

Pain And Hardwork 117

The Turning Point 131

The Boomerang 149

The Last Chapter 159

Acknowledgement 175

*"Destiny is something that puts you back,
whenever you try to escape from the script of life.
So, enjoy the success and failures of your life
and love the way it is."*

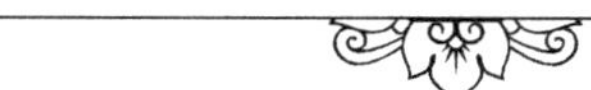

INTRODUCTION

Hey, I am Durgadas BR and I am from god's own country "Kerala". Writing a book was always in my dreams since my childhood but first I thought of writing this book "ISHANA" when I was in the first year of my Engineering and that was a holiday and I was in my home. I opened my Facebook account and created a page in my name "Durgadas BR". The topic for this book "My Dream Girl" was in my mind for years. So, I just started writing it in my timeline with whatever the shit came into my mind first. After posting a two- three-page thread of my story, I waited for people to put their responses.

After 2 days, I started getting responses for the chapter "My Dream Girl" through messages and comments. Amazing story, so realistic, is this your story, such kind of responses made my message box full. I became so happy because I was not a good reader nor a good writer. My English language is not that great and now also I used to get trouble finding suitable vocabulary, sometimes.

After a few days of appreciation and suggestions, I thought of writing the complete book but I couldn't write more than 10 pages. In one or another way, everything seemed boring for me and I understood that this is not the right time to write a book.

I slowly became inactive and messages and comments also getting lower but within that time, I gained nearly 2.5K followers. So, I didn't delete the page and I thought, I could use it when the book is complete. After a few weeks, again I started getting messages from some people who already messaged me before. "Is your novel complete? Where can we find your book? Is it available online?" such kinds of questions popped up multiple times from multiple people's but even if I tried a lot, I couldn't move to a single extra page.

They understood that I am not going to complete this story and I also stop replying to the messages that come on my page. Then I get busy with the other things of my life and the second time I thought of rewriting this story was at the first year of my MBA and that was a great flop too.

Now when I look back, I understood one thing. That I used to write this book whenever I felt the most depressed or sad. Writing something, even though I was a bad narrator makes me so special and I was like getting a new purpose in my life. In the life of Prajwal, he may find the purpose because of his "Dream Girl" but for me "This book" is my soul purpose. I had tried to incorporate my timeline with that of Prajwal but the story base, events, and characters are pure imagination, and if there are any similarities with the people you know! Then it's pure coincidence.

I have a lot of things to tell you but I am not a legend in literature nor a pathetic writer. I was someone very normal who writes! Just like a person who can chats pretty well with his friends on WhatsApp or Telegram. By becoming a writer what I am seeking is for you! Listen to me so that I could understand you and connects with you. This line may sound a little like 'Nithyananda' but never mind. I just want to be a part of everyone and wish to know what's my soul purpose in this world, for you.

PROLOGUE

Before you start reading this book, you need to understand that this book is not a regular love story. This is the life story of an average middle-class Indian and his life full of love. You may feel this story is a little fast-paced because this story is happening in the plot of approx. 13 years of time and half of the story will be trying to portray the character of Prajwal and his lifestyle. so kindly take it in that sense and Have a great experience with this motivational love story!

"Love" is one of the most amazing things in this world and lovers, they are the hero and heroine of a mesmerizing world that they create for themselves. Mostly Love will never start with both people loving each other, but firstly it will put the spark on the one, and then he or she will hold it for so long in their heart. Whenever a situation comes, that they feel like they can't hold it anymore. It's time, they will look for a way to express the love that they had locked in their heart for so long.

The most amazing part of any love story begins from here. They will do anything to make their love success and they will go in the weirdest routes that no one will ever go. During that time, they will be like a thinker who always starves for new ideas and they will be a poet who writes romantic poems in their heart and they will be a good human who starts loving, even the minute things around them. That they would never know, even been existed. A bird's song will get to hear different; flowers will get beautiful than ever and even nature feels romantic. If you start seeing things in a more elegant and lovable way then that means, you are in love.

It's not hard to get love to become a success. If you can love someone more than anyone else in this world and you are ready to go to any extend without excuses, then your love will get successful but if you failed by any chance then don't blame destiny but blame your decisions.

Always remember that not all are successful in their love. Laila- Majnu, Romeo- Juliet, even Lord Krishna and Radha, all were perfect examples of divine love but they couldn't make it into marriage or the success that we see in the love stories that we usually share. Just love deeply and enjoy that feeling, let the time decide what's needs to happen.

From this book, you will understand how all destiny can play with a common man's life and some good insights about leading a heroic life in which we are the judge and we will grade ourselves. After all, self-actualization is the highest level of psychological development that anyone could ever achieve.

1

PRAJWAL

First of all, you need to know a little about my life before knowing my love story. I am officially being called Prajwal Virendra Varma but, I would like you to call me PJ as I don't like to pronounce my name by myself. I am an engineering undergraduate from a university in Kerala and an MBA graduate from a university in London. Here becoming or trying to become an engineer is the easy and least spiked path. Also being the child of a typical middle-class Indian family, engineering and medicine are the pathways to success.

In my case, no one forced me or asked me to go for engineering but I was automatically engineered in my mind that I want to be an engineer, from my childhood itself. May be due to the influence I felt in some of my elder brothers in my family who already became an engineer or even some movies that motivates me a lot. My father was an EX-site engineer and my mother is a teacher that makes me a kid of an educated family. Moreover, No one in my family ever questioned me in the decisions I took in my life. So, where I am standing now was pure because of the decisions I took in my life and a mere destiny.

Here is the real thing I want to share with you. If you are reading my story means you are connected with me somehow and destiny is the only thing that makes you read this. I don't know whether you believe in destiny or not, but I do. Whatever is happening in our life is just because of the decisions we took in our life and pure destiny. We may think we are taking decisions intentionally but if you look deep, you will understand whatever happening is going in a flow and what you are today is a projection of how good or bad you handled the work assigned by your destiny yesterday.

We don't know where we will end up or what we will become and who all will join along with us, in the journey of our life. There is no visible future and the memory of the past is not going to help us in present. There is only one time and that's present. Destiny had done its part in the past, will do in the present, and will be going to do in the future also. What we have in our hands is the skills and attitude to handle the job given by our destiny. Even if it's a failure or success, cherish it in your ways.

In this world, the only things we can't cherish are hunger and bad health because, without good health and a good meal to eat, even the most successful people in our eye can't say "I am blessed". Our success first starts when we start our life in our mother's womb then when we are born, when we first talk, when we walk and the series of successes goes on till our death. If you are reading this means you have successfully studied how to read, how to understand, and how to think in your imagination. All these are basic standards of human beings and animals don't do all these things, aren't, they successful? They are also successful in their life, in their standards.

So basically, you can't determine other's success until they participate in the same competition as you are. I said this because the priorities of every individual are different. You may give more value to money, materials, or luxury but it may not be the case of someone else. So, if I don't have what all you succeed in your life that doesn't mean I am not successful because I may have succeeded in many things that you may not. One becomes unsuccessful if he becomes unhappy because happiness is the real reward of success. If you and others think someone is successful and if they are unhappy, then you should rephrase it.

A person who cherishes his failure is the one who succeeds in the pain of failure and he who is the most fortunate because someone who can stay happy during their failure can't be succeeded by anyone who puts imaginary standards for other's success.

If you look into history, the biggest heroes don't need to win a race or a war to become the champion or a leader. Respect, happiness, and dignity came from our good deeds and not from our better results. In my life, I don't usually care about other's respect but I always focused on self-respect, and that I even showed in my love also. Even in love also you don't need to impress anyone to become successful but being selfless and divine is enough to get the feeling of success in your heart.

Love is like a miracle; it can make you do many things that can't even be imagined and even a wimp can become a hero if someone is there to love and motivates him.

Somehow in my life, everything I ever achieved is because of Love, a truly selfless love. You will understand everything after you come to know my story completely. Keep loving everything and everyone so hard that not even a stone could resist you and you will also learn it for sure, from my story.

2

MY FIRST INSULT

People may have insulted us many times but we don't remember all. Maybe an insult that is verbally much sillier will be hurting us more than something bigger, that even done with very bad intention. You know why? It's because that silly insult is something that is aligned with our destiny or our self-respect. For example, in many English movies, we may see people calling each other "fu***r, Mother-Fu***r" etc. If someone calls that in Kerala; Surely, he will get an opportunity to consult a dentist for repairing his lost tooth during the fight. So, for each individual their values are different.

In my case, the first insult I felt as an insult has happened when I was in my 4th grade, studying at Green valley public school. That's the time, my father got a visa to Dubai for his new job and we were going to relocate to my mother's house in a little faraway place in Kerala itself. It was nearly the end of the march which means the current academic year was going to end and our class teacher Miss Kelly asked all of us regarding "Who all are going to change the school this year". Many students started saying the name of the school they are going to join and she was appreciating their decision regarding joining a tougher syllabus than they were now.

When the rush is over, I stood up and said with excitement "Miss Kelly, I am going to join Whittle public school. It is a CBSE school that means it is tougher than our current Kerala State syllabus. I was expecting an appreciation for that and She weirdly looked at me and with a pity expression, she told: "You are not even scoring any good in-state syllabus itself and if you are going to a national syllabus means a sure failure".

It's the worst experience as a kid I had ever encountered from a teacher. Even though I was not a good student, I never think 'I am lesser' than anyone in this world. She could have told like "You need to study well to survive there, I know you can do better" or something like that. As a teacher what she said is purely not fine but these kinds of insults are the fuel that fire up our inner drive to destiny.

After my 4th grade, I went to Whittle public school for writing the entrance to join there and I successfully failed in the examination. It's the time, I felt like what she told me was true. My parents also come to know, "what my old class teacher mentioned about me in the class", because I cried in front of them saying about the insult, that I couldn't endure. "I am not brilliant ma; I can't study this kind of tough"- I told to my mother. They could have made me join another state syllabus school nearby my current home but they believed in me more than I believe in myself. They make me join Staten Central School (SCS), which is also one of the prestigious CBSE schools nearby.

I need to specially mention Staten. It played a major role in transforming my life, my attitude, and my views about everything. It's the place where I understand and experience many first things in my life. Maybe due to the past insults or due to some good tuitions, I scored an 85% mark in 5th grade where normally I used to score 50 - 60% in the state syllabus but it last for only one year. I again changed back into normal as, below-average student. It was always easy to change back into normal when it comes to studying and I wonder changing back to normal in any other things is this easy?

If you ever get an insult and if that insult is keeping you motivated to do something, remember that insult every day. Write down your pain in a book and read it again and again. Use it whenever you need that as motivation. If you forget the route you came from, then time will take you to the places you came from. So, a man who always remembers the bad routes he came from and the wrong decision he had made, is the only one who could better understand a new route he is going to travel now or in the future.

I forget the routes I came from in the mirage of happiness and overconfidence that I created in the new atmosphere. So again, I started circling my old life and I started becoming lazy and lazy and lazy. Success is like a spark; it may make a fire or may not. sometimes just fire up a little and make some useless smoke. It's not about spark actually, it's all about what is burning. If it's water, it will not burn. If it's petrol, it burns so vigorously and if it's a plank of partially wet wood, it may burn a little and end soon. I was like that plank, who fires up a little due to the spark and ends soon as I didn't cherish that success enough. I got insulted, I succeed in that insult and then I forgive.

Forgiving is good quality as many legends say but in my life experience, we don't need to forgive always if it is purely giving a positive impact. Because revenge in the form of success is the best thing, we can always throw to the face of anyone whom we hate. Making someone's negative words false, is one of the most interesting games we can play in our life.

Everything will happen in your life according to

destiny. If you never experience any insults, it's great that you don't need to create a situation for an insult to happen or even wait for it. If something happened by its on, cherish it and use it for your success. That's what I meant. Most of us will worry about the failures that we already encountered and waste our time that we could use for something productive. Even the one who is brave enough to end their life would never think about leaving their life for something useful, not by ending but by bravely facing even the deadly situations.

You may feel my stories so silly or even irrelevant but I am taking situations that are pretty relatable and would have happened in your life also. I would like to make you understand very simply and I don't want to flabbergast you with gigantic stories nor with confusing jargon. Life is a complex phenomenon and if we look deep into it then we would find everything as a joke, including us. So, it is not necessary to believe in hard thoughts and complex stories because even a rabbit story is enough to understand the complex things in this world. Whenever you start looking at things in a very easy way then you can find easy solutions for the most difficult problems in your life. If an exam can become tough for you which is easy for someone else then even the problems in life will be like that as it's all about how you are seeing the problems and remember you are the one putting standards for everything around you and don't allow anyone else to do that.

3

MY DREAM GIRL

s I said in the beginning you may or may not believe in destiny but in my life, destiny played some amazing jobs. It just happened when I was in 6th grade. Till that time my life goes quite naturally but that day makes a lot of change in me. Just like every guy of my age I also feel some sort of attraction to a girl, but "what special from others is" she is only my 'Dream Girl'.

Every day she comes into my dreams. She sits beside me, talks with me, and even laughs with me. That makes me start loving nights more than my days. I patiently put away the days for my beautiful nights. In this way, my three years have been gone and I have become a 9th-grade student.

From my childhood, I like to read science fiction and magazines. One day when I was looking through the pages of a magazine, a face suddenly strikes me. With no time I identify that she is the same girl who comes into my dreams because I can't forget her beautiful eyes, sizzling smile, and floating feathery hair. Moreover, her face has been already scribed in my heart.

Is that hard for finding an angel even if she is in a crowd? No! So, I just find her and I just put the magazine off and start dancing and jumping like a crazy monkey as I at least found 'she is not only my dream girl but also living in the same world that I am living'. My happiness at that time where uncontrollable and my cells and body become super energetic than ever and at that time, I felt I could lift 100 kg.

After some moment I eagerly pick up the magazine and turn to the page I see her. It's an article concerning student's findings in mathematics, one of the craziest subjects I ever hate in my childhood. I read each word in that article carefully. Hurray!!! Finally, I did find her name.!!.

"Ishana" my dream girl. I said her name along with me just like a 3-year child studying a word.

"Ishana. Prajwal" it's matching too. I thank my mom for putting me in such a name which is very much matching with her.

I take her photo from the magazine on my mobile cam and keep watching it day and night. My love for her keep increasing day by day and started to think of how to get her as mine. This gets affected my studies and my failures in examination become my partner, everyone started asking me "what is going on in my mind?" teasing from my parents became my daily routine.

At last, I understand that "just dreaming and simply watching will not gain me anything" so I decided to take some strong decisions, for that, I need some perfect planning. I spend the next few days on life planning. It's crazy that a 14-year boy planning about his life. But I don't take it as a matter, I just make a perfect plan. As a part of my plan, I decided to study maths as it is her favorite subject. So, I started going for extra classes and spend much more time in studies than dreaming. Even I put her photo that I cut off from the magazine, in front of me as it's the only motivating thing that was leading my life.

Days passed and my 9th-grade annual examination has started. Every day I go for examination after seeing her and the day will surely a wonderful one after seeing her smiling face. At last, I completed my 9th-grade examination and it's the time for enjoyment!! Yeah, my vacation has started. In this vacation, I have some plans in my mind which have to be done. I heard girls love music, as my voice is not so sweet, I quit singing and join in violin classes as it is the master instrument that makes strong feelings in mind. I am a little bubbly at that time, how a sweet girl like her gets impressed by a bubbly guy like me. So, I started going to a bodybuilding center for making my body strong and fit. Sometimes during the pains in my hard work, I even think how crazy I am for doing these kinds of things for a girl I have never seen in my life. I don't even know where she is? and what she is doing? or do I ever get a chance to meet her? These all thoughts make so many cracks in my mind but I never give up.

I strongly believed that every hard work will surely give the result. I know God will surely give me some way so, I continue to work with my plan. After one month my 9th-grade result has come and I got 90% marks in all the subjects. Now everyone who teases me has started to say good about me. They don't know that the reason behind my success is Ishana.

Life is like this; we don't need a real reason for success. In my case, Ishana was just a reason that comes into my dreams for transforming my life. In your life also there will be a person or a thing or a dream that motivates you every day, a spark that burns up at all times we need. If you don't have one, look for it and keep hold of it. Because without a specific reason what we achieve is just some random success. The goal of the winning team will be highlighted more than the losing team. In life, every success is like a goal, people will cheer hard but if you fail as a human then all your success will go in vain and nothing to do with the winning part of the game that our life offers.

In our life also, we will encounter so many successes

but if we can't align all that to a point of bigger success it will be good for nothing. We may have seen highly educated people who wander jobless. For them, they have a lot of opportunities in their front and they will get diverted or distracted by many paths. But for a guy with only school graduation, opportunities will be less and during a hard time in their life they will be open to all the openings in front of them and they will understand their true potential in their journey of life. But in the case of highly educated people, they are so choosy and, in the end, they will stand with nothing in their hand. So, what I am saying is don't get highly educated. No! that's not what I am saying. I am telling you, even if you get highly educated or you are a holder of many success! without having a proper vision of what you want in your life, you will stand in the middle of nowhere which is very complicated to figure out at the end.

Now the question is how to figure out where you want to go? That's a very simple task. Be open to everything and explore new things in life when you have enough time. As a kid, you can make many friends, play a wide variety of games or talk about or hear about everyone's interests, do new tasks, participate in events and say yes to every opportunity that comes into your life. Even if a chance for cleaning the public place comes, just go and do it. This kind of open mentality will make you understand your limitations and strengths. For example, if you eat a wide variety of food, you will come to know what all things you like to eat and what all are allergic for you and even you can make a better decision when you are alone and in a faraway place. There are many situations in my life I went to new places alone and got a food allergy. Because in my house, my mom used to decide what food to cook and what all she cooks will be suitable for me But I was unaware of what all will not be suitable. So, exploring and experimenting a lot will make you an experienced decision-maker even though you may get hurt during the process many times. Notice one thing, explore new things along with a group always. Because in my life experience, groups make us strong and learning from other's mistakes is also a good option. Also, a group will always back you up when you got into trouble.

You may have seen many quotes saying "Those who are weak, follows the group but the brave walks alone". This is good to say but the literal meaning of this kind of quote will not help us in any way. You need to look deeper into the meanings of quotes because most of the quotes have an inner meaning but people always interpret them all in their standards. Walk alone in the sense means to choose the road that is less taken. Following the group means, going beyond what the majority is doing. We must be brave enough to choose the path that is less taken but having company during the adventure is always good. If you look into any adventure movies or some epics.

4

NEW BEGINNINGS

My 10th grade is the most memorable day in my life. During my 9th grade, there is a piece of news came that the CBSE is going to end board exams for 10th grade and they will be evaluated by the school itself. There is a common talking that, the folks who change their school from CBSE to State syllabus after their 10th grade can score better in their 12th graduation so they will get more weightage in Medical/Engineering entrance examination. Now they are telling, there will be no board exam in 10th CBSE so there arises a doubt regarding whether we can change the school after 10th or not. So, my family decided to make me join a government state school in 10th grade itself so that I don't get any difficulties while applying for the admissions of a state syllabus school after my 10th grade.

Till my 9th grade, I was studying in private schools only. Clean buildings, regular and punctual faculties, neat dressing, English talking, and home works, are the world I had ever experienced at that time. Even I didn't get to talk with any girls, much in my life other than asking for a pen or an eraser while in need. My first day in the government school itself was like a fresh book with complex jargon for me.

The school was nearly 100 years old and our classroom was the oldest building I ever visited in my life. As it's a new beginning I came a little early into the class and students started coming one by one and in groups. Everyone looks at me with a pleasant face and asked my name and details. A new experience that I gain from there was, it's the first time I talked with that many girls in my lifetime, other than just asking for a pen. All are super friendly and the class atmosphere itself was very energetic. It was like a typical classroom in government schools, that I have seen in some movies.

In my older schools, we used to wear shoes, ties and be skirted all the time to look like a gentleman, aah more like a gentle boy or girl. Whatever! Here there is no need to buckle the shirt nor need to wear a shoe or tie. Here I saw people in their most genuine form because they all have the freedom to dress like a CBSE kid or as a normal state school kid. So those who buckle shirts and wear shoes are the ones who wish to be like that and those who don't care about all these pieces of stuff are the ones to be like that.

Days passed and I also get along very close with many people there. They became a part of my life and I started laughing and enjoying my life in the most affordable way anyone could ever imagine. Here we don't need to give a treat for our friends to please them nor need to go beyond like a dog to get noticed. Here all are the same and people with the same tastes are Broz for life.

The common talking about the CBSE to State syllabus thing seems true. It was a little bit easy to handle the scenario when we are coming from a tougher syllabus. Teachers seem the same everywhere, here also I got some good teachers and they were genuine in their profession also.

While I was in other schools I used to go to school, just for the sake of studies and even I used to sleep during boring lectures. Here in this new school, I got some new opportunities to explore a lot. Even if it's about my friends or about the activities we share. I started going fishing with my friends during the weekends and we used to play football in our PT periods. Even I got some girls as my best friends also. All of this was a new experience for me.

You may feel all this as silly because you may be doing all this in your day-to-day life or you may have to get used to all of this. But it's not about the activities we do, but it's all about the freshness we share in our life. I am telling all these silly things to you because I want you to know the secret behind my happiness. It's a proven fact that people can't stay happy with the same happy life for a lifetime. Even if you are extremely happy today and you are encountering the same situation or similar things for the rest of your life, how will you feel? Do you feel the same extreme happiness as today? No! you won't. The most beautiful 'sentence' in the world "I LOVE YOU" from a person we adore will not be that beautiful if they started telling that to you every day, for the rest of your life.

Now! I am not telling you to change the person in your life, for getting new experience. Nowadays, the majority of the relations get to break up due to boredom or lack of love. Where did the love go, that was at the extreme once? That doesn't go anywhere but with you itself. It's all about what you guys share in your life which makes you feel boring or even fed up. If you don't feel happy with any person, whom you love the most before! try to figure out what's the problem between you guys. If you can't figure out a specific problem, then the problem is your life itself. Try to change your life by changing the routine and try to accommodate new things in your daily schedule. Like! "Go and watch some movies, if you don't use to go", "Drink tea instead of coffee if you were drinking coffee daily", "Switch the tasks you were doing, like if you were doing the cleaning and your partner were doing the cooking, switch among yourselves".

By understanding the other person's difficulties in their lives and sharing new experiences with them, will create some new beginnings in your life! Even after the worst days, you shared. So, in my life, this new school itself is a new beginning for me. Even though I was happy with my old school too.

Actually! you don't need to wait till it becomes worse, to set new beginnings in your life. You can create some new beginnings always, to keep you fresh and rejuvenated. In my life, some new beginnings come by themselves just like you or anyone could encounter. You may also have experienced many new beginnings by yourself!

Another new experience for me is my love at first sight. All of you have this kind of teenage crush experience where you fall for someone at first sight itself. In my case, I was standing outside my classroom during my interval and suddenly a girl was running opposite in my way. She was like jumping and running like a deer. There is this beautiful smile on her face that just makes me stand still and enjoy that moment for a while. I have seen many girls in my life, maybe some cute girls, angry girls, beautiful girls, average girls, or whatever. But she is a little different, I can't say she is cute because she sounds a little weird and loud which is not part of cuteness but I just loved it. She always used to jump everywhere like she was doing jumping jacks, It's kind of cute Maybe! I don't know. She was a little chubby in her face but she is not fatty. Her body is fit and perfect for a beautiful teenage girl. Simply I fell in love with her. Whenever she comes in front of me, a Tamil kuthu song will beat inside my head because she is a power pack.

You may have wonder what could have happened to my "Dreamgirl", Now that's the twist. After few days I felt guilty because when I was nothing and when I was sad, "Ishana" my Dream Girl was the only motivation in my life. She was the first girl who took place in my heart. When I started loving this new girl in my mind, I started to watch some random bad dreams during my sleep. I don't know what was the reason but I felt guilty about what I was doing. So, I stopped crushing around her and try to avoid being in her presence. Her name is Mariya Johnson and she was studying in my same grade but different class. Even though I had a crush on her, I never told to anybody and now it's over too. It was like one beautiful dream that doesn't last long.

I had a picture of Ishana in my purse and after I got that picture, I lost the connection with her in my dreams. But still, I value her more than anything and whenever I think of her, it was like a great motivation to break the limits in front of me. As a boy, it's common to get attracted to anybody but love, it's a different thing. Even though when we say "I love you" to someone, it may not be that strong in our minds. We will get to know the depth of our love when we get into commitments and reality. If we can say "I love you" to the same person with the same feeling after completing a long 5 or 10 years of the relationship, then we can confidently say "I love her". Just like that loving someone for a while and moving on to someone else too fast is a symbol of weakness.

We don't need to fill the gap of someone who is no more in our life or for someone who is not filling the gap we allocate for them in our heart. In my case I love Ishana but I don't know where she is right now and what she is doing. Also, I don't know whether she will love me back in the same depth I am loving her. I had done a mistake loving someone else in the middle without even giving a chance to Ishana, the girl who made me what I am today.

That's why I avoid loving the girl at the beginning itself even though I had an infatuation with her.

Days passed quite happily and I also nearly forget about Mariya. One day I was sitting on the last bench during my interval time and one girl who is a friend of mine come to me and asked! Hey, I heard something that you are loving Mariya? I got shocked hearing that because it was a very secret in my mind, I didn't even share it with anybody or not even my best friends but how did they come to know. I hiccupped a little bit and asked her in a confused voice! Who said this non-sense? "that all we know."- she replied.

After that incident, no one asked me about that nor I think about it. Days passed and one day I noticed something that whenever I cross near Mariya, a light kind of laugh burst out from her friends. I understood that they also come to know something But I wonder how they all get to know, what was just in my thoughts only. Usually, if we love someone, everyone in this world comes to know except the girl we love. Here the thing was a little bit different, it seems like she itself comes to know it first and she must have shared that doubt to her friends also, I assumed.

By the passing days, this news spread everywhere and everyone comes to know this including some lecturers. I became a little popular in my class, I guessed. As I was a new boy to the school and time doesn't go much to create any kind of hatred, I was like a good boy kind of person to everyone in our batch. Maybe because of that, everyone was so enthusiastic about my love. If a thing becomes viral as a piece of news, it becomes truth by itself even if we resist. In my case, I didn't know what I need to do because what all others are saying is true but that was before only and now, I stopped seeing her in that way.

She started getting shy whenever she saw me and there was another boy in my class that loves her so much. So, my friends even conduct a poll that who should be her lover? You know what! I won the poll with a 99% vote. Look how funny the situation is! A guy who truly loves her got zero support, and a new guy like me to the class, who just felt an infatuation towards the most energetic girl in the batch have full support from everyone and the irony is, if we start thinking about not getting something then that will come to us even if we try to throw it away.

One day a street drama is getting conducted in our school, by some guys from outside and we are watching it in the auditorium. Suddenly a friend of Mariya comes to me and told: "Mariya want to tell you something, can you come to her?". I was quite sure that it was something related to the love story that is going viral these days. Even though I was a little nervous, I act confident and slowly walk towards her. When I reached near her, she smiled at me and just walk away saying nothing. I looked at her friend who took me here and they started laughing at me saying "If Mariya calls, you will come anywhere Nah!".

I felt really bad, I just take it a negative sense that they were fooling me. I slowly walked away and one girl came to me and said "Don't you get it, bro, she loves you". I thought she was trying to make another fool out of me, so I told: "Oh really! then go and tell her that I won't love a girl like her, she is jumping here and there like a little monkey and I don't like such kind of girls". That was the biggest lie I ever told in my life, even though it was from my anger. I loved her because of her energetic body manners. She was like a battery that spread positive charge only. But even though it's a lie or truth, I said no to the love she may or may not have for me! I am not sure about that because only her friends told me that.

After that incident I noticed, she is trying to avoid face-to-face contact with me. I never see her jumping here and there, after that. She changed a lot afterward, which makes me feel really bad about what I had told about Mariya to her friend that day. I thought of saying to her personally that I love the way she is before but then I thought it may worsen up the situation more because I don't like to play with the emotion of others. Maybe because of that incident, some of her friends come to me and said that I have missed a wonderful girl in my life, I don't know whether it's true about that missing part but she is a wonderful girl as her friend told me.

After few months, the guy who loves her proposed to her during valentine's week and she said 'YES' to him. I felt happy for them because somehow, I was sure that the guy who proposed to her is sincere and he would not hurt her in the way I did. After Valentine's week, the month of March came. What special about March was that it was the last month of our high school and after that, we all are going to different places.

We all bought an autograph book and started sharing our memories of each other on the beautiful pages of it. My book goes through the hands of everyone and finally, it reaches Mariya. She wrote something in a long paragraph and closed the book and ask me to open it only after our high school graduation. I couldn't even express my sorry to her before, so I promised her that at least.

Final year's exams came in few days and the countdown starts for the last days of our high school life. Everyone started hugging and crying to each other that it will be a big missing after this and for me also I had changed many schools before I never felt this sad because this school was like a new world for me, a world that is full of love and happiness.

As it was the last day, I decided to tell sorry to Mariya once and for all because I don't know whether we see each other again or not. I came looking for her and she was standing with her lover and talking, she was crying and he also looked so disturbed so I thought of not irritating them at that moment. They may be sad that they are also going to get separated for a while. Anyway, I was happy about her for being in a happy relationship.

So finally, the school was over and I also started moving on thinking more about my higher studies and my focus was completely on fitness and future goals. Higher secondary will be a crucial part in deciding my future and all that I have in my mind was doing something great which adds up my qualities before Ishana comes to know about me. I am not sure where Ishana will be now or whether she has a boyfriend or not, but I prayed to God every single day to keep her single and make her impress in me when I get to see her.

One day I was purchasing some kinds of stuff from the market and I accidentally met "Dheera" the name I didn't mention before. He is Mariya's Boyfriend. I was so excited to meet him because after the high school graduation I never met anyone in person. I enquired "How is Mariya? What are your guy's plans?", he became silent for a second and told don't you know that we broke up while we were in the school itself." I got shocked! "When, Why, How?" I couldn't hold my thoughts, I never expected this because when the last time I saw her, they were together. "We broke up during the last day of our school, she said she is not interested in love and all so it's better to break up than wasting our time in love"- he said. That's insane, I couldn't believe what he told me. I didn't talk much with him after that. I got disturbed after hearing their breakup. I was thinking it again and again but how could she break up with a guy this early, if she doesn't like him why did she accept him in the first place! Thoughts started jingling in my mind. I lie down in my bed facing the shelf and I saw my diary over there. I slowly read the pages from the starting of my new school days. Each memory scroll through my mind. When the pages that I have written about Mariya come, that Tamil song started playing in my head again "Dheem thanakka thillana dheem thanakka thillana. Thee pudicha nila naandhanae". The rhythm of this song still gives a feel of her energy in my mind. I don't know why! Some of my thoughts make multiple emotions in my mind. I close the diary and put it on the shelf back and I noticed my autograph book was lying there, dusted in a corner. That time I remember the promise I had given to Mariya that I never open her page before my graduation. I scroll directly to the last page looking for her autograph.

What she has written in that book, just breaks me into tears. "I saw love in your eyes once. Even though it was short, I could cherish it forever. I changed my attitude for you, I tried to make you jealous out of by promising love to someone I don't love but you didn't care. I don't want to know the reason; why you can't love me anymore but I will love you forever and ever, No one can take that place in my heart, other than you".

After that, I don't know what to do or what to say. Now I don't even have her contact nor her current status. The only thing I understood was that even with or without my knowledge I played with the emotion of other people, either Mariya or Dheera. I tried to find her for many months, just to say a deep sorry from my heart or just an apology for all my mistakes that I ever made to her but I couldn't find her.

"Life is like this" once what is done, is done and sometimes we can't even think of re-fixing it."

Our future is the consequence of our current or past decisions. I don't know Mariya is a loss for me or not and I don't know whether it's just part of my destiny. That Mariya's role in my life was becoming just a distraction from my love towards Ishana and by losing her 'I proved my dignity or desire or foolishness' whatever it is that the time needs to prove. I didn't feel any regret for losing her love but I am feeling regret for making her worry about something that doesn't even deserve her. You may feel that I am disgracing me but I don't know really!? Whether it's me or anyone else, we don't have any authority or greatness to hurt someone who loves us because love is something that can't be bought with money or anything valuable to the outside world. You can buy friends with money, you can buy pleasure, luxury, and even family but on the micro-level the love that comes on its own! can't be bought nor created.

It is true that I only love Ishana and for Mariya, it was just like an infatuation that lasts not more than few days. Even if I start loving her for sympathy, it's like cheating her and I don't wish to do that. I tried to forget that matter believing she would soon move on with her new acquittances and friends in this fast-paced world.

5

TIME

During my 12th grade, That's the time I got some exposure to new opportunities and fresh minds. One movie just inspired me that time, "3 idiots". It's the story of a Mechanical engineering student and his friends and the hero of that movie was selfless, brilliant, and study things because of his love for knowledge. I was studying things just to pass the exams and I don't have an idea what I was studying too. Someone told us before that whoever controls media, controls us. It makes sense when this movie motivates me a lot and I strongly decided to become a mechanical engineer one day. I also thought, if I become a mechanical engineer like the hero in the movie then My Ishana will be so proud to be my girlfriend. Assuming everything is the only option available for me so what else I could do for my Ishana, as of now.

I was not a movie buff till that time and actually, I watched that movie by accident. It was the time I got a new Android phone and we all come to know about Xender, an app that can transfer files so fast. Till that time, if we want to send a movie then we should transfer to a computer and then from computer to our mobiles, very tedious task, isn't it? Anyway, the things like Xender made our life easy and because of that I even get a film accidentally which makes me decide to study engineering.

In our life, some decisions we take will be so stubborn and it will make us end in somewhere we never thought of. I joined an entrance coaching center for preparing for my engineering entrance exams and slowly I understood, nothing can be achieved in a day or a week. Months passed but my confidence level gets low due to the negativities around me. For joining reputed colleges like IIT's and NIT's, we need to qualify for some of the toughest entrance exams in the country. I strongly hold on to the dream of becoming a mechanical engineer and finally, all the entrance exams got over, and unfortunately, I didn't get qualified in any of the national level exams. I became really sad and it was like my dream almost gets over. But in India, we have a cheap alternative that we can join any of the private engineering colleges if we have money in our hands. The fact is that the engineers who got out of such kind of colleges are mostly good for nothing and if we throw a stone into the air from India, it will certainly fall into the head of such an engineer.

Anyway, something is better than nothing. So, I started enquiring about all the private institutions in the country. The first college I visited was Imperial college of technology and advanced studies, which is nearly 50km from my home. During the time I visited, it was under construction and I didn't get a really good feeling. After that, I visited many colleges inside and outside of Kerala. After every visit, the infrastructure and appearance of colleges started getting appealing to me. Within that time, State engineering entrance results also came out and I registered for online allotment. The irony is I got selected for the college, which I thought I would never join for whatever reason. Yes! I got a government seat in Imperial. As I got through the entrance, the college fees were much lower than the management quote so finally, I made my mind somehow for becoming a part of that college itself. Maybe this is called destiny, sometimes we will get what we least expect and even least likely.

My college is very new and we are the first batch who got admitted to this college. Things are a lot harder when all of us are into a new atmosphere and we are going to be the system. Whatever we create will be the benchmark for the coming batches and what all culture we are going to portray is going to be the culture for at least some more years.

We felt proud sometimes and at the same time curse ourselves for the decision that we took as we need to suffer double than the students from an experienced or a much-reputed college. While we are telling our college name to our relatives or any old friends, no one heard about this college and also there is a high risk that we will end up having no placements at all.

We were the seniors and we are freshers so we lost many experiences being ragged or bullied by our seniors nor we have a role model or a specific culture to follow on the campus. In the beginning stage, we are confused about all these things but later we understand what all negatives presiding here, have a strong positive side too. We were the leaders and every corner of the campus is going to tell our name. There won't be a single space that we didn't use in the first place. As we are the first batch, we would have a special place in the heart of our management too because we joined there trusting them and they will try to do best for us also, everything is just part our business, isn't it?

6

ROYAL MECH

Apart from all the struggling part about joining a college, that's the place where we enjoy our life to the core and that the time, we do the weirdest things we could ever imagine about. From the ending of teenage till the beginning of adulthood, our blood will fire up with energy hormones that can make us a king or would burn us and destroy us into ashes. It's all about the decisions we took by intention or by an unintentional motive, whatever it will be that it's going to cherish us or going to haunt us for many years to come.

I started college with only one intention is to Study well, score good and get placed in a great mechanical engineering post but even I know that this kind of intention won't last long. College starts with an induction program where all branches sit together and it was like for 3 days. Several games and interactions created so many friends among us. After the induction program, we all got separated into different classrooms based on the branch of study.

In the beginning, this branch separation just felt like a family separated in different rooms but by-passing months students get to develop the politics of being in a separate community. Like Royal Mech, Civilians, etc. the name goes so weird but the motto is unique that everyone wants their branch to be powerful and best. I don't know whether in any other countries we could see this kind of nepotism in the colleges! because here from the day we were born 90% of parents are telling their children to be an engineer or doctor and in engineering colleges, there are separate branches and that creates a fu**ng opportunity to raise their hormones and start a fight. If the situation is like this among a small community itself, then there is nothing unusual about countries fighting each other! It's in our genes.

I am a part of mechanical engineering and what special about the mechanical branch is that it is the only branch girls don't prefer to study and that's the main thing that attracts me also as I won't get distracted from loving my only love 'Ishana'. Also, it has a masculine image and in this first year itself, we were like 50+ boys in the class that will add up more than the total of boys from the other branches which makes us the strongest clan in our college. Others will dare to raise, even a fight against us.

With all this politics and disproportionalities aside, some of the boys from our class got committed with the girls from other branches, especially from the civil. If we don't have anything on our side, we will take it from the other side that was the universal rule and war after that! Quite normal. They already divide among us, now we just need to conquer. Most of my batch mate's love story was like that and that's the reason which creates the first fight between the civilians and Royal mech too. They came as a group of 20 or 25, which is the assumed number of complete boys from the civil branch and we were like 50. When the fight begins, Civilians started running to places where we can't find them, and finally, only two of their leaders who assembled the army left to receive all the punches. Our guys punched them to the core and their faces look like rotten tomatoes after the fight.

I never get into such kinds of fights in the name of branches. I always felt this like pretty non-sense because either the fight will be in the name of a girl or the name of leadership. If someone is really good enough to be a leader why should they fight to get that position and about the girls, even the history proved war in the name of a girl will destroy everyone.

I don't want to take a hit in my face for some random girl who fell in love with my friends and I don't care about any of the other girls in my college too as in my eyes 'Ishana' is the only girl I want to care about.

Whatever may be the reason, this kind of silly fight starts getting interesting and funnier as there is no criminal level of things ever happened. Everything just ended up in a couple of punches or a few foul words. Other than this kind of silly fights there was nothing much in our college to enjoy, as only a few of us were there in total and many competitions were among us and that's doesn't make any excitement. We itself get bored of competing among ourselves.

One other special thing about college life is the Hostel and it is the most amazing thing in our life, where we use to live as a family full of friends. Till our school days, we may be with our parents and friends are just someone we use to get hang around during the interval time, whom we sit along with or someone who just gave us a company during the weekends but when we get into the college, they are our pillar of support and they will be with us for whatever shit we want to do and we will also start doing weird things along with them.

7

MY ATTITUDE

My attitude is something that is not preferred by others. Maybe due to my experiences in life or due to the stupid way of seeing this world from a different perspective which made me a boring personality. I am a selfish kind of person but that doesn't mean I am unempathetic. I was selfish in the sense, I don't usually put my head on others' matter, and mostly I was an inward-looking person who used to talk very little and always used to think a lot that maybe something related to life, the universe, Ishana, or even something weird. I am a person who is interested in a wide variety of subjects which makes me a good listener but my silent personalities always push me back from the extrovert friendship lists.

In many famous quotations and thoughts that went viral in the media; what they may have taught us is to be unique, for becoming popular or being loved by others. But there is a slight change in its literal meaning from what we usually assume. Being different means, you should do things that others prefer, in a way that they never expect! for becoming a well-respected personality. For example, just think about bill gates donating one million $ to charity and a kid trying to collect 1000 $ for charity. The kid will get more news value than bill gates but benefit wise what bill gates done will be more useful. Also, if bill gates wear a white shirt worth 1000$ and we wear a fancy shirt worth 200$, people will say he is simple and see us like a person who relies on luxury and Do you ever see someone calling an upper middle class or middle-class wearing 10$ plain shirt as simple? They would rather see them as poor but won't say simple so basically, certain terms are only for those who are doing things differently in the way that other's want. People don't always care about the value but they will praise things that they least expect from you.

Just like that, in my life also my attitude makes me a less valuable person among my friends. I used to love them sincerely and do whatever they ask for; like If they ask for a treat, I will give them. if they said something good about me, I will blindly believe them that they are always good to me. If someone asked me for help, I will do it even putting off my priorities. If you give out something so easily to others, they will not value you because they may feel you like the bill gates donating to charity as even a big help from us will be just lower than what they expected from you. People will get mistaken by the easiness of getting and they won't see the beautiful mentality behind that giving or the sacrifice we have done for that maybe our time, money, or even our unfinished works. This is the reason why attitude girls have more fans than a friendly girl in our colleges and this is the same reason why good girls fall for bad guys. You may wonder what's the logic behind that but it is true because bad guys say lies to girls and mostly don't respect them. For getting that respect and making them truthful, they will try their level best and be better. In the case of a good guy, he will always be truthful to their girl and they will be very caring to them than they could ever expect and which will make insecurity in the mind of the girl as they will be always under the arms of an overprotective man who even protects her the people that she believed as her friends. For them, what they want is already in their hand and that doesn't make any further thrill or anything unusual or interesting to do afterward and even irritating sometimes by getting more love than they ever expected.

Maybe my good boy attitude makes me a boring personality and no one ever care about impressing me because they already know that I am going to be helpful to them whenever they need me. If someone of your friends comes to you only when they have a use which means you and I are in the same category.

One day I came to know about the problem of my attitude. When I get into a small issue with one of my other batch mates, there I didn't find a single guy to argue for me but many people who used to come to me when they had a need once are strongly arguing for the guy in my opposite. That's the time I understood, don't help anyone expecting anything back and only helps! if you can forget it. We can help anyone feeling pity due to empathy or even sympathy. This may be the reason, why rich people won't help people around them but they will help people whom they don't even know. One very good example is our country itself. We may have heard about India donating crores of rupees to Other countries for eradicating poverty just to tighten the friendly relationship among them but India itself has many people who suicide due to hunger or poverty. The farmer suicide is not at all breaking news for us, it was just part of an old tradition.

After that incident, I became a little more conservative and selfish. We all need to be a little bit selfish in our life to become the fittest to survive. History also proved this many times, for example, if you look into the Neanderthal man and homo sapiens. Neanderthal man was much stronger than sapiens but what makes sapiens survive over Neanderthal man and rule over till this time is their selfishness. Sapiens took more than they could even accommodate and exploit whatever in front of them and their power of gossiping create a sense of planning before destruction.

If a monkey took a bunch of bananas that he couldn't even eat and not sharing with his friends or acquittance, our scientists will study and will get confused over why the monkey is acting so weird. But if some sapiens took 90% of the wealth that is not at all useful for them and leave others to work for hunger, we will name them as highly successful people and put their pictures in front of the Forbes Magazine.

I am not saying being selfish is good because that what the rich society is doing and what makes the problem is them being selfish and we middle class and lower becoming too kind and selfless. If everyone is selfless, this world would have been a paradise. Anyway, that's not going to happen and what we can do is get along with the fittest. You can become selfless once you don't need someone else to become selfless for you.

One such incident happened in my life during my first-year university exam. Our first exam was mathematics and It was so tough for me but I managed to write for 45 marks. My friends asked me just like everywhere else that what all I have got and I said I got the answers for three questions with 10 marks and some short mark questions and I enquired to them also. All of us were looking for a benefit that we could gain from the other one and unfortunately, I had a benefit of 2 marks and they had a benefit of 10 marks from me. We normally need 40 marks to pass the exam and I had attended for 45 marks only, that also not sure. In such kind of situation bartering a 2 mark for our 10 marks is a very valuable deal. So, I asked them to show me the 2-mark answer first and after that, I will give the 10-mark answer, I promised. They may feel it bad but becoming a little selfish during exams is not a bad thing. After all, we are competing among ourselves though.

After that incident, they started seeing me as a selfish man but when the result came, they all scored like 41,42, etc. and I scored 40, which means I just passed and have a lesser mark than them. After the result, they thanked me for that 10-mark answer. You see, here I didn't alter anything after my past doing of becoming a little selfish in the exam hall. I have given them what they want for still they blamed me as selfish rather than thanking. This is the real world outside. Everyone wants support from you but if you ask for something in return, you will become selfish. The help I offered them made them pass the examination and at the same time what I asked in return saved me at the border strike. After the result, they also forget everything and move along with the new things in life. If I thought about being selfless and avoided asking that in return, I would have failed in that exam and they would have also felt sorry for the guy who helped them pass the exam. But that doesn't go to make any use for us.

Nothing is confusing in this but for selfishness also there is a good deed. In my attitude being selfish is not making someone else suffer but expecting something in back or maybe I can say "NO free help please". As I told you earlier, I will also become selfless once I don't want anyone else to become selfless for me. The only thing I used to do selfless was loving Ishana, without even have a scope of getting it back but I expect a little that someday she will also love me in the same way that I do. Some people have one rule for them and another rule for others but in my case, if I am saying something, that is applicable for me too. That is, I don't want any free help from others too, I will surely give something useful in return. I feel that's the most dignified way of helping each other and in the help, we don't need to rank which is lower and which is higher, we just need to think whether it's useful or not. That's it!

8

JUST PART OF DESTINY

After the results came out, I understood one thing that Engineering is one of the toughest things to study. The pass percentage in the class is like 20%. In our school days and all, it's very rare to see someone fail in the final exams even though we didn't study much for the exams.

By god's grace or due to good luck, I had cleared the first-year exams in my first attempt itself. That gave me a lot of overconfidence and free time than usual. So, I thought of doing some new things and what struck me first was going to the gym. Our college was a little strict as it is the beginning, we need to take permission to go outside the hostel after a certain time and that just made me feel like a prisoner all the time. That was irritating to take permission all the time so I took my roommate along with me to the principal's room and ask permission for going out every day for the gym but he said 'no' without even thinking a shit! I got so pissed off hearing that, I went from there telling some foul words about him in my mind.

On the next day, notification for the university sports meet has come and our sports coordinator ask us to give names for the events. I was interested in athletic events but one event that I never tried in my life, just lights the bulb in my brain. "Boxing", yesterday I asked the principal regarding the permission to go to the gym but he said no. Now I am participating in boxing, so he can't resist me going out for training. So, I gave my name for boxing and took permission from the same principal itself, who rejected my request yesterday with his stupid monkey face.

I had no interest in boxing so I simply go out have some good food, and enjoyed my evening with some chilled beers while sitting in the serene climate of the rice fields which was very common near my college locality. It just went like that for some days and one day our sports coordinator asked me regarding my progress in the training and I said, 'sir, as of now I am just doing some ground exercises and some weight training', I lied.

He may have noticed the lie in my eyes, so he asked me to come to his friend's gym which has a boxing club along with it. In the next day itself I went to the gym he said and some of the guys were practicing in the ring already. Our sports coordinator was also standing there, he introduced me to the boxing trainer. He gave me a handshake and said you will surely win the tournament, I got flabbergasted. I weirdly looked at him for telling such a lie and he asked me to do some pushups. I started doing it and that goes on like 10,20,30 and he was not asking me to stop. As they were watching me, I also go on with the flow in his counting. It goes till 78 and my hand started getting pain. So, I stopped myself without waiting for his command.

He gets inside his cupboard room and took red color gloves with a white-knuckle area to me. He put in my hand by himself and I can't explain my feeling at that time. I felt very special wearing that, it's like I got some extra power in my hands. He started demonstrating to me the different punches, "This is a jab, this is straight right, and left hook, right hook, etc...." The next few weeks were so hard as I got to pass through some vigorous training in my life. I was weak in controlling my emotions and always feared getting hurt by others, whether physically or emotionally. So, I used to be an introvert sometimes, selfish other times, and most importantly I don't take anyone too friendly. But after that training, I became emotionally so strong that I got a belief that I could defend myself physically and that confidence automatically improved my emotional strengths too. I wonder! whether my queen 'Ishana' is going to get happy? if she comes to know her hero, is officially a trained boxer now. It was like a miracle, that I started taking life much simpler and sillier. She must be lucky, that her lover is a cool and calm guy now.

You may have wonder, why someone needs to boost his story about being silly, we all had taken life silly many times and all are doing it. What special in that? Almost all brilliant minds would have asked you to take life seriously. Your parents, friends, or even Gf/ Bf could have asked you to become a little more serious. But in my opinion, two kinds of people take life silly and simple, one is the stupid people and the other one is the strongest minds but those who take life too seriously are the fearful people, they are the ones who always worry about the future, worry about losing what they have, worry about getting hurt. So, what they do is, becoming serious and plan to defend fore coming events.

These people who take life seriously are the most dangerous for this world. They will kill animals, cut trees, and capture lands saying this "we need to conserve land for our future generation as they will also need that to build houses to survive". This is what the historical sapiens do till the 20th century. Now it evolved and people start investing from their life and money from the younger age, working day and night while sacrificing all the enjoyments in their life for the sake of their kids and for getting secure during their retirement period. When they get secured and started feeling the joy of safety, they would have reached their mid-50's or 60's and they believe they are living a confident life because of the hard work they had done before. But actually, what happened is that they get old and that confidence is just part of the stupidity that they have done in the name of getting secure. The people who take life more seriously would always worry about every simple issue and escalate it to higher levels. Suppose if your boss, at work, don't smile at you back and you are a serious-minded man. Then you will find many possibilities for that like 'he is angry with me', 'My previous work may not be satisfying', 'Maybe he is planning to fire me'. Seriously some people will think to this extend. It's the level of seriousness you took in your brain that determines how miserable you need to lead your life!

What all else! In this f**king world, everything that is expensive is a contribution of this serious-minded common man. I said common man because rich people are not at all serious, they will stay cool and use the serious people to struggle for them. Gold, platinum, diamonds, all these things; people won't wear daily or we could rarely see on some occasions but everyone has few or a lot of this. In India, every woman would have a collection of this. Someone would have been attracted to the color or the sparkle once and maybe during that time, these things are rare too so people who had money, started collecting this and make it unavailable to buy. But years passed and millions of people started living in this world and if everyone thought of buying a coin-sized diamond each, then also there will be enough of that quantity to supply. But by the ever-increasing rate and seeing the seriousness of man, they keep on increasing the value and at a point, people started getting unaffordable for that. Now the things which were just a product in the past centuries becomes the most valuable in the present world.

Suppose if everyone has all the diamonds and gold in this world and no more to sell by a miner or by the shop. Then it will become a possession like a demonetized currency that stopped printing but the government has permitted to roll among the public itself at their own risk. Now you can either wear all the diamond and gold in the public or you can barter it with something else. As I said, it will be like a demonetized currency that slowly diminishes value on its own. After all, it's just a metal that has some amazing properties, maybe some companies will take it from you for putting in some kind of chip or something else, and then if the rate increases by any matter, they would substitute it with some other alloy or artificial things. So basically, all the problems are creating by us and will sacrifice our lives in the name of getting secured! All because of their weirdest fears. Always work for your happiness not on things that the economy tries to implement on you. Money, real estate, Gold, Diamond, all these kinds of things have value until you believe in it and if you start not believing in all these materials and start working for your happiness, then your life will unfold straight to infinity with a lot of time and abundance.

I may have told a lot of rubbish things in my story but you don't need to follow any of my thoughts or ways because we both are leading different lives and as I am telling from the beginning, be good and do things that are beneficial for you with no bad intentions and if someone got hurt by any of your actions, try to compensate always. Just like Jesus said, those who understand their mistakes will be forgiven. Lord Krishna also used to tell something "Goals are important and not the path, but always keep good intentions". That what I am trying to follow in my life.

Anyways back to the story. After some vigorous training, the day has come for my first trial match. They measured my weight and I was 60kg so they put me in the lightweight category and my opponent was a steel-bodied man, who was so lean but strong muscles visible as cuts. I was a little nervous as it is my first fight and I didn't even engage in a college fight nor even received a punch that hurts.

Fear triggers my adrenaline but I managed to get back my confidence in the next second itself. When the ring bells, blood starts heating and the sound of friends cheering and the ambiance around the ring put my brain to a silent mode for a second and get back into the senses. I middle blocked his right-side punch and aimed for a right-side punch back, leaving the left hand low and when he thought of punching in the left side, I put a middle block again and had given a strong jaw at my luckiest moment. Down! he was down that simple and I never expected this as an easy win. That just proved to me that sometimes luck is more important than talent. Here he doesn't lose because he is not good! He is a good boxer but the time was favorable for me so I have done well. Anyways, that just boosts my confidence to the next level and even helped me winning the University and south level competitions even though I was not at all experienced as all my opponents.

The national-level competition was held in Mumbai and It was near my 4th-semester university examination which is just 2 months ahead. So, I decided to quit for this time as I have got a surprise gift in my 3rd-semester result just after my south level tournament. I got failed in 2 papers! Even a bad or a good thing, every day was one or in another way gives me the shocking news. Slowly my overconfidence becomes a little less and I started focusing on my studies again. After all, without graduation how I am going to find a job and search for my Ishana and how she is going to get impressed by me. Maybe this boxing is just a part of my destiny to make me learn some new lessons in life.

9

FACEBOOK

One day evening, I was just lying in my bed and scrolling through the Appstore. Then by mistake, I clicked on the Facebook app, and a page where review, ratings, etc. was opened. The first review just strikes me, "Very useful app, I found my old best friend through this". I had used Facebook once in my 12th grade and after that, I didn't use it because the data charges were so high. Now they were giving 1 GB for 200 rupees. So, I also thought of downloading it and check whether my friends are there.

I created a new account and took a selfie from my hostel itself and put it as my profile picture. Tada! All ready to explore. I clicked the search friend tab and there was an option to find friends by suggestions. As I had updated my college and past school details, they started showing me the profiles with similar info. Many of my old friend's profiles start popping up and I felt so happy. It's like a nostalgic feel that roams in my head and I started giving friend requests to each and every one on the list. Within some minutes some people start accepting my friend request and for the next few days, I was in the thrill of getting back my old friends.

One moment, I got an idea of "why should I search for Ishana in this!" I typed Ishana in the search column and many profiles started popping up but I couldn't identify which one is her. Most profiles have the picture of flowers, Cats, birds, etc. I don't even know her surname or place or anything other than her first name which made me pissed off. But I didn't give up. I started sending friend requests to at least 5 Ishana's every day and wasted my time talking with the wrong people.

One day when I was sitting in our playground watching my friends playing badminton and waiting for my turn and I just started scrolling FB in the middle and searched for Ishana once more and I couldn't believe my eyes for a minute that her profile popped up in the top itself. I closed my mobile for a moment, clearing my eyes and controlling my happiness because at that time It feels like I had found the multiverse or invented the Time machine.

I got one thing cleared that if you want something in your life, it will come to you at the right moment.

But you need to patiently wait for it. Now I have all the confidence in this world to find her one day because now I can see her on social media or even become her friend in a day or two, I guessed.

I again took my phone and opened her profile picture. She changed a lot but her beautiful smile and that feathery brown hair are still looking the same. She was wearing a red jacket, seems like she took that while doing some kind of trucking in Manali or some other parts of the Himalayas. She was standing there like a cute angel in a red color dress where the snow and the beautiful mountains add extra beauty to it.

I send her a friend request and started waiting for her to reply and by that time I got all her profile details by hearted. Her location was not mentioned and most of her posts were private. So, it seems like I am not going to get any personal details of her for the time being but I come to know that her favorite movie is "Devil wears Prada" and she loves to read books in which her favorite is "Looking for Alaska" by John Green. Until that time I don't use to see much of any English movies, other than spiderman or superman, and reading novels was not in my dictionary especially fictional stories. But I ordered "Looking for Alaska" online that day itself to know her taste.

One day was over, two days were over, and it goes on like 3, 4, 5, etc. and finally, I decided to send her a message before even get accepted. I opened her profile and started thinking about what to message her but as time passes, I got afraid and I left that plan and then I started looking at her profile once more and started scrolling her timeline and there was nothing other than some shared mems and videos. I scrolled till the end and I saw something useful, her school name! Yeah, finally I found the school she studied, hurray! And it was like another info about her, into my dictionary! My mind sparkled.

I searched her school on google and comes to know that it was an international school in Mumbai. So, "she must be a North Indian girl"-I said in my mind! Yeah, she even looks though and the second thing is that she must be rich for studying there. That makes a little disappointment in me as I am a middle-class south Indian guy who doesn't even have enough money to spare for an iPhone that I always aspire to buy someday. But seeing the phrase I phone here, don't get confused because I can't afford any other phones either. If I want to have a new phone, I need to tell my parents in advance, that also in 1-year advance at least.

It took me a lot of time to get my confidence back but I come up with the idea of adding that school in my profile and search for her old batch mates. I proceed in that way and started sending requests to random peoples, I don't even know.

At first, no one accepted my friend request but after few days one guy just suddenly accepted my request, and after that maybe by seeing mutual friends' other people also started accepting my friend request. I started messaging people with Hello! And How are you? Some people asked "Who are You By the way!", "Do I know you?", "Why are you messaging me?", everyone is asking all this at the beginning itself and that just ruined my intention to know more about Ishana. All of them were so conservative and it was pretty unfamiliar for me as we normally used to socialize with strangers while we used to travel in public transit or even while walking through the streets. I felt it a little arrogant and attitude kind of thing. But later only I come to know that this kind of question is just normal and some other guys started asking "Who the F**k are you?", what the F**k you want? I got pissed off and I replied "I am your father" for god-forsaken.

You know what! Anger is not the solution to anything and when it comes to love, we should be extra patient otherwise you will also get into trouble like me. I created a bad image among some guys whom she may know and I started noticing many guys unfriending me for no reason and I am pretty that the guys which I got an issue with, started doing their part. Rumor or gossip, that will spread much faster than a forest fire and once it starts, we can't stop it by any means. It needs to be forgotten by the damn time.

I got a sure idea that I messed up everything. If she was of my age the students of the 10th or 12th grade must be her juniors for sure and even maybe her friends or neighbors too. Even by accident if she comes to know about this then She is going to block me for sure or been put on her blacklist. So, I decided not to complicate things anymore.

The next day morning when I was scrolling the notification tab, a message popped up "Ishana accepted your friend request". When I clicked that I got reverted to her profile and at that moment itself, she just removed me from the friend list. It's true that Facebook was just an application and getting friendship in that is not a big deal but that time getting the feeling about "she seeing my name and looking at my profile picture" before accepting the request takes me to Shakespeare's level. Many things started pampering in my head. It's like a feeling of touching her for the first time because she has responded to something I put forward and it's a kind of virtual contact, isn't it?

Weird! But still, I would like to cherish that moment forever even though It hurts me like hell.

"Ishana" the dream girl who always comes in my dreams, whose face which I cut from a silly magazine that I put close to my heart. After all these years, she just rejected me in the first contact itself, when I get a chance to connects with her. It breaks me into pieces so I went to the bathroom, open up the shower and put a piece of loud music on my phone, and cried for like 30 minutes.

I got depressed after that incident and it was like all my dreams just shattered into the dust. But I don't want to lose my hope for this simple matter. I am way stronger than this, my soul tried to convince me. So, I started thinking, what to do next! And different ideas come to my mind like drinking some alcohol and making my mind fly, getting committed with some other girl without bothering about the past, and many other shitty things that I don't even want to mention.

At that moment I got a text message from my sports coordinator, "Do you made your mind to quit for the nationals? This kind of opportunity you may get only once in a lifetime so if you have any change in your mind, please text me back". That message was like a message from the guardian angel because I was confused at that moment and I had no idea about where to channelize my sorrow and anger during that time.

"Sir I changed my mind from yesterday itself" I texted back instantly before he gets to change his mind. He may also get excited hearing that because he would have never expected to see someone changing his mind this fast. Anyways I started my training section again and there were only 15 days left for the tournament. I could have started this before itself but what can we say, life is like this. This kind of situation makes me feel that we are living in the script of someone else because here also I took one decision and, in the end, what needs to happen will happen. Maybe I can say I am the one who changed my decision and take up this opportunity but in actuality, the opportunity chooses me and I was just a part of the destiny.

10

B FOR BOXING

My event is going to happen somewhere near Kandivali, the North Mumbai region. My sports coordinator has a friend in Bandra so he arranged a room for us in "Grand Residency Hotel", nearby Bandra itself. Mumbai was a very busy city compared to my home town. Huge buildings, porch cars, modern dressings, that's the moment I started feeling my dressing style and taste need great improvement.

While I was walking through the streets of Bandra, I saw a Starbucks coffee shop. They don't have one in my state so I never get a chance to try one from there. I saw this brand while scrolling through the timeline of the students from Ishana's school. So, I decided to take a shot, I ordered an espresso from the menu, and the bill was surprising 135 bucks+ taxes! for a regular coffee kind of thing which tastes very similar to the coffee that we get from a local shop in Kerala for 7 or 10 bucks that also without any taxes. You know what! The difference between rich and poor in India is that rich people will buy kinds of stuff wrapped in a luxury cover that a poor used to buy from a local shop that just doesn't have a cover, for 10 times lesser price than the riches pay. In the end, the things which add luxury to the products went to the dustbin, and rich or poor, both will be happy for satisfying their needs.

The surprise for the day doesn't stop with this. While I was crossing the road, one car just passed in front of me. BMW 320d 3series, I am more specific in the car model because I am a mechanical engineering student and luxury cars were always my weakness. Yeah anyway, that car was not a surprise! the person who is sitting in the car was the surprise. It was 'Ishana' in the car, who is sitting with a lady who looks like her at first sight! probably her mother, I guessed. At first, it was like a dream. I didn't understand it for a moment. The car went so fast and I didn't know where it was gone but I was damn sure about what I had seen because of her face, I can even identify her in the crowd of a million people because it's always inscribed in my heart. I came there to do something impeccable to forget her but now time brings her in front of me again to pull back all the bloody memories I want to forget.

Now itself I was completely down knowing she is a rich girl! And already I lost my dignity in front of her and her juniors who rejected my friendship on Facebook. I felt bad to proceed with her because I felt too low in front of her that I don't even have a car in my house, I don't have a bike of my own either and even my weekly pocket money can't make me confident enough to enter a Starbucks that the people in her community may drink daily. My subconscious mind was not ready to listen to my consciousness, it just started looking for her everywhere when I was walking through the footpaths of Mumbai. I went back to my room; I was really tired from the day so I went to sleep a little early.

The next day, I went for a short workout section with the selected candidates from the south whom I have already been friends with during the south boxing meet.

Finally, the day begins with a bang! We went to the tournament spot and completed the formalities and checkups. The match was starting in the evening only. People were warming up and getting ready for the evening event. There will be 3 rounds and 8 participants of the total, 4 from pool A will be competing with the people from pool B and the winning 4 will be split up into two pools of 2 each and they will be competing with each other and only 2 will goes to the finals which will be the first and runner up.

I wasted my time here and there trying to avoid looking at my opponents practicing because if I may feel them as stronger than me if I come to see them working hard for the match that may kill my confidence. Anyway, I can't improve anything at the last moment and whatever going to happen, let see in the ring! That was my attitude.

The tournament starts and all the contestants were asked to take the lot. I got 2 and they asked all the evens to be in pool B and all the odds will be pool A. So, I am going to participate against pool A and they said looking at pool A, "fight against your double". This means contestant 1 is going to fight against me in round one. Pretty shuffling, I got a north Indian white guy with almost 6 feet in height and the only relief was that I am in the lightweight category so he is not going to crush me anyways.

The bell rings and as usual, I got blind in the fear of getting hurt, hormones ooze up and I started defending in the first minute, the specialty about me is that my reflex gets faster and stronger when my body heats up so by defending and taking up some no point punches will make me charged up for some powerful kicks. Just like all the time, when the right moment came, I started punching him in the stomach and face without giving him time to settle back. Bell rings for the first break and I don't imagine that is going to be a break in my heart too. I saw Ishana cheering up for my opponent from the audience's side. Now just like in the films, my eyes turned into a DSLR camera and my focus point was Ishana and in slow motion, her mouth cheering for my opponent and asking him for kicking my ass off, everything silent and ting, the bell rings again for the next round.

I got out of focus and I couldn't concentrate on the fight. It feels like I f**ked up and fear, anger, sad nothing was there I got emotionless for a few seconds and I felt like running

off from there. Anyway, it's not possible so I need to finish it fast. I loosen up my defense, so I got some punches in my face and stomach and I noticed the joy in her face. I always dream of seeing her smiling face and now also she is happy. For a moment I forget about keeping her happy, kicked him with whatever energy I have and didn't give him a single chance to take a score and at the end of the match, I won with the maximum score.

After the score, I was not happy about my winning but was sad about her cheering for my opponent. She is my dream girl and I want her to see me in the same way I am seeing her and none of my expectations is happening in real. I saw her hugging the guy after the match and he also put his arms around her waist and walks outside. It's the worst feeling any lover could experience. I am loving her and she allowed someone else to put his arms around her waist. This may be common in English films but I can't just simply take it in that easy way. I started realizing how possessive I am to someone I love.

It was like a man with a broken heart who got struck by a lightning. I am already depressed for getting rejected by her on FB and now seeing her hugging a boy and caring for him. The Mannerism just proved to me that he must be 99% her boyfriend. He also looks so handsome and rich which makes a perfect suit for her.

I felt like teasing god for doing all these things to me. I was born in the middle class and genetically I am not a charming guy as well. But okay! somewhat good looking that's it. I would have simply lived my life just like any of my friends but due to my dreams and my dream girl! Years of planning and the mind castle I build now got bombed in a single day.

Maybe due to my distracted mind or due to the hard punches I have given to her boyfriend, my knuckle got a problem in my second match and I got out of the tournament. Pure waste of time, I could have simply sat in my hostel room and read out some books for the exam. Now I am mentally and physically broken and I don't know how long it's going to take me, for getting over it!

I dressed up for all the patches in my body and take the next morning flight itself, to Kerala. Because each second, I spend thereafter that incident was killing me inside and I was in serious need of patching up my mind.

When I reached my hostel room, it was like I got my heaven back. I focused on sleeping for the next 2 days and physically I get back to normal. But mentally I couldn't get back into normal. Crying in the shower doesn't make any sense to me anymore so, I started smoking along with my friends and tried to keep me away from the unwanted thoughts about her. Now I got completed all the bad habits! I drink and I smoke.

Once when I was weak and blind towards my future, she comes into my life and lighten up my soul and took me till engineering and even I have made some victorious achievements in sports too but now I failed everywhere. I got failed my exams, tournament, and my long longing love. I believed she was real, while she was just in my dream only and then time itself proved that she is real through that magazine and now I had found her with my own eyes and she was just in front of me for hours but I couldn't even say hello or just a smile at her. My love becomes a failure, isn't it? Even before getting a chance!

11

GAY-DIAN ANGEL

I t took me 3 weeks to get out of the shock and another shock was waiting for me, the university exams. I somehow studied at the last moment and write the exams with some passing scope. So finally, the second year was also over. But this thing always runs through my mind "You are a fool who loves a girl for all these years, just to see her along with someone else", this kind of thought just irritates me.

After the exams, I went on some trips and tried some new dishes from different places. I don't know why?! If we are really sad and if got something delicious to eat, at least some of us would forget our worries for a while. Some call this kind of people as stress eaters and I would like to call them a foodie. I started taking non-veg items every day and that made my 20 days semester break, an amazing experience for my tummy at least.

My college reopened and I also started engaging in entertainments like smoking and drinking. I was aware of the consequences but I couldn't get rid of it which I started after one or another depression. You know what! People started smoking in school because they are curious about knowing how the addiction feels like but if someone starts smoking after he joined college, then it must be either to show their manliness or due to some kind of depression. Drinking is also a bad habit but it does not have a specific reason to start mostly it gets started in some kind of friendship parties. As I am always saying media controls all of us. In movies, the hero used to smoke for showoff, and sometimes he smokes some extra cigarette when he is depressed or angry. These kinds of portrays are ruining the youth. On the side of films, it will show smoking and drinking are injurious to health and hero must be smoking on to the screen fascinatingly. So, what a normal youth will imagine, heroes won't die of smoking. When are they going to portray some heroes who die of smoking at the end and heroine ran away with the villain? Whenever the theater starts showing the biggest hero choking and die of smoking in the "No Smoking" advertisement they put at the beginning of the movie, then only people would understand that smoking would even kill a hero. Now they are simply showing some waste fellows whom we can't even relate with us and how can they even imagine that we would change smoking seeing these guys. Do you think that the one who put the "No smoking" advertisement doesn't know about this? Then you are stupid because they are the same people who studied the fact that only "Influential people can impact you and not someone who comes in the No smoking advertisement." After all, everything is just a part of the business, isn't it? So, it's your business to stop smoking if you want to live happily and die happily.

Now coming to my story. If you take the life of me itself, I was devoted to my true love towards Ishana but what happened at the end is, she saw me as a villain who hit the ass out of her hero. Probably, she would have thought "F**k man, go to hell!". But I am a man with self-respect, as I don't get her that doesn't mean I hate her. She will be always in my heart and I am not going to love anyone in my life ever. Jai hanuman ji; the lord bachelor, I started to become a devotee of him and tried to control myself from all my addictions, weaknesses and for giving a new path to live for. It's really funny that people will start praying to god only when there is a problem and we will think like "I am going to change completely, no one can ever break me again, I will get invincible", even we may do a couple of push-ups every day to prove ourself, that we are strong and will get stronger but again after few days, old things get to dig up, open by itself and ooze into our memories for poking us in our oblongata which makes us dizzy again and we will feel like "Ooh man! Why life is like this?" and slowly we will get weaker and weaker.

When I was a kid, I was much stronger than this that I took almost all small insults as fuel to my revenge of success but now I am in feeling to forgive and forget. I didn't understand when did I become like this.

Finally, after all my thinking, I decided to burn all the memories of Ishana that I have. I took the cutting of her photo that I have in my purse. I lighted the cigarette lamp and with a half mind, I put fire to her picture from a corner and when it slowly burns into ashes, my heart started feeling blank. Then I turn to my mobile, took the gallery, and deleted her profile picture that I downloaded then I take my Facebook to delete my account. Like the last time, I checked her profile and clicked settings to delete it, and just before confirming I got a message on Facebook, a notification popped up. I thought of deleting the Facebook without looking at the message because it must be any other message like "who the f**k is you?". But I get so anxious and Thought of reading the message one last time and delete it afterward. I go to the messenger and it was someone named Rohan Ferranti. What a shitty name! but it's a "Hi" in the message. I go to his profile, a weird-looking guy with a sparkling brace on his tooth. He is studying in the same school as Ishana studied. So probably he must be a junior of Ishana, I guess. I replied to him "hello".

"How are you?"- Ferranti replied.

I got shocked because it's the first time, I got a reply like this from a guy from her school! All of the others were either rude or very private.

"I am fine, thank you", I replied.

He replied with a smile emoji and the conversation goes on with basic information like school, college, our home town, etc.

He was studying in 12th grade there and after getting a little close with him, I gathered all my courage to ask him about Ishana.

"Hey, can I ask you something"- I put a message

"sure, anything bruh!"- he replied. He was a very fast replier. Always used to get a reply in minutes or even seconds.

"Do you know Ishana? She must be your 2-year

senior I guess!"- after messaging this, I eagerly waited for how he is going to react.

"I am not sure bruh, I know one Ishana but she is of my batch"- he replied.

It must be not her anyway but just for curiosity I asked- "Can you show me a picture of her?"

He replied to me with the picture and I got shocked. It was the same Ishana and I was confused too! How come she write an article which had a difficulty level, even a 9th-grade student like me couldn't understand that time, could be written by her in 6th or 7th grade that time probably. Surely, she should have copied just like me for doing the assignments or someone would have helped her. How foolish I am that I even struggled a lot to study math, sacrificing the sleep for many days, and what all rubbish I assumed with that article! I need to become brilliant to impress her and vaquero Valera. SHIT! I bite my hand to suppress my embarrassment.

"How do you know Ishana"- he asked!

"I don't know her I just saw her in mutual friends so just asked"- I lied.

"Yah! She is a pretty girl; everyone will notice her quickly"- he said.

"Oh okay! Nothing like that, I just asked that's it"- I said

"It's fine, she is single. If you want you can love her"- he said

I felt weird and at the same time so happy because I thought she is committed and there is no point in loving her but now one guy is telling me she is single!

"How do you know that? And why are you telling her details so openly"- I asked in doubt.

"She is my friend dude and I also know her very well from 7th grade."- he replied

"Okay then, why don't you love her?"- I started testing him with my questions.

"I can't love her bruh!"- he said

"Why?"- I asked

"I can't love any girl"- he said

I got confused. Maybe he is also heartbroken like me. I guessed.

"I don't get it, why? Do you have any breakups?"- I asked

The chat got paused for some minutes. He was online and started typing but even after 5min I didn't get any reply but he was still typing it shows. I eagerly waited for his reply because I want to ask many more questions. He was like a spy I got there in her school. He is in her class and now my friend too so I would get all the details I guessed.

"I am a GAY, Bruh!"- He said

What the heck! You are typing a single sentence all this time, I thought he was typing some kind of story. I got pissed off!

"So what bro, we all are Guys! What's the problem in that?"- I replied

Again, after a few seconds pause:

"Not Guy bruh! I am a Gay. It means I don't love girls; I love boys."- he replied.

My eyes bulged outside, Wtf! I never heard of a boy loving boys in their life. Maybe due to this, he may have talked this sweet to me, again embarrassing. I don't have any more space in my hand to bite, I looked.

"oh, okay bro! fine."- I replied

"Don't worry I won't bother you; I already have a boyfriend."- he said

He started giving surprises to me again and again like this. I wondered who must be his boyfriend and how the fuck they would have fallen in love with each other. I wonder! Whatever he has will be there with his boyfriend also. So, what would have attracted him to love another boy? My doubts started getting bigger and bigger in my head and my stomach starts paining so I calm up my mind and get relaxed after few minutes of silence.

As he is gay, I got confident enough to tell my love story to him. I started saying my story from my 6th grade, about my dreams, how I find Ishana for the first time, how I get her profile on Facebook, and how all these friends from her school and even him get connected to me. Finally, I told my incident at the boxing tournament and the way she looks me with hatred.

"This is so touching bruh! I feel like crying. Hey! She is not committed to that guy at the tournament. He is her cousin, Rayan!"- he said.

Oh, my holy crap! now it makes sense, he must be her cousin's brother that's why she allowed him to hold her in that way. I felt bad about thinking negatively about her. What all I thought was just wrong, now also she is single and good as always.

She is still single and now I have a helping hand who is very near to her which means I can get closer to her which means. I got back my full confidence, more than ever before.

12

SPY REPORT

After understanding the depth of my love for Ishana, Ferranti promised me that he will help me getting my love successful. I became so happy that I never expected, my life would turn around like this.

He started explaining to me about her hobbies, her likes, dislikes, her character, etc. From what he said, I understood that she has an amazing voice and she loves to sing songs. She is the kind of girl who talks so loudly and that feature of her reflects in her talents too. She sings the song in Opera and one video Ferranti gave me was just amazing. She is an amazing girl with a full package of all the talents like dancing, singing, acting and what else. She loves to debate and above all, she was friendly to all and very down to earth.

I know that she was an angel who was born on this earth by mistake and what I imagined about her was true and accurate. I started feeling life as a script because all things happening around me were like a miracle. I was like a one-man army and now Ferranti was the first one that joined along with me in the battle of my love. At first, it was a little embarrassing for me to keep a friendship with a guy who was confused about his gender. Then I understood, it is just a hormonal disability and I thought, this kind of guy understands our feelings more than our privileged genders.

In our place, if a boy gets more emotional or cries like a girl will be teased like "Are you a Shikandi, to cries like this", which means transgender. There is a stereotype in our community like men can't cry and get emotional is the symbol of femineity. By hearing these most men, suppress their feelings and in the end, they even became incapable of understanding the feeling of others, especially the feelings of a woman. That's why I said people like Ferranti can understand people more, they have the guts of a man and emotions of a woman.

After knowing her character in detail, I started seeking to know more and more about her. By knowing her better, I started getting so addicted to her and feels like I could never live without her and even I felt that my soul purpose is to love her and serve her in my entire life.

What's the purpose of knowing her details when she doesn't like me! I started thinking of ideas about how to start a conversation with her and by what means? I got really confused.

Without knowing me! how she will love me or even going to talk with me. On passing days! I started feeling, all these understandings about her and the help of Ferranti is not going to help me for anything. I can't ask him to take a chance for me to talk with her because I was like a stranger to her and he won't do that too. She is his friend and if she comes to know he is helping me with her updates, it will create much more problems than I could expect.

My 5th semester was almost over and I got busy with my exams. I almost cleared everything which I want to know about her and also, I have nothing else to talk about with Ferranti. So, that just put a full stop to our chatting. I decided to take a break in this matter before taking a specific decision because I was so confused about what to do next. Within that time, I cleared all the supplementary papers that I failed in the last semesters and focused on my current semester. After the exams got over! I started reading a lot of books related to love and watches a lot of movies. In whatever I see, I was searching for a similar kind of situation in my life but I couldn't find anything useful for me from anywhere.

If I do something like cinematic, like in movies going directly to where she is and roam around her, disturbs her and make her miss me when she doesn't get to see me. This kind of thing is not at all possible in my life. I don't have any money to go there and suppose if she calls any police or someone, my destiny would end up in jail also. It would be wonderful if all of our life becomes a movie, where we can be a hero and even if we get arrested, heroine itself will bail us out and even fall in love for us by becoming sentimental. In my case, Ishana doesn't even know me, and if I try to go in the path of creating emotions or sentiments! Then also, it won't work because she won't even give a face to listen.

So, I thought like becoming someone, no girls would ever reject! Like Hrithik Roshan or Justin Bieber but neither I know acting nor I have a masculine body and most specifically I don't sing or dance. That means I don't have anything she likes.

I started trying acting in front of a mirror to check whether I could act because if there is any chance like that, I would become a famous actor and stand in front of her, I guess! but my acting was horrible. So, I tried singing but not even I could bear it. Dancing, I couldn't even try. Then I understood my thoughts were going weird and stupid like this. If becoming an actor or a singer is the qualification for her love then she would have committed with someone who does but 'she is still single' isn't it!

Then I realized that for getting my love back the only thing I need to do is to make her understand how deep I am loving her. Suddenly I got an idea of writing a book that if I could convey how all I am seeing her and how much she is in my heart! She may get a spark of what I have to her. I got fix with that idea and starts writing my feelings through poems and songs but destiny hits me there also. Maybe I am not destined to be a writer that's why I couldn't express the same depth, how I feel about her and how much she means to me.

So, whatever spy report I got about her and what all planning I put in my mind! Everything just went into vain but still knowing her this much and my imagination about her, worth a Kohinoor diamond that is full of life and I could cherish it for my whole life.

13

THE FIRST AND LAST

Time is like a race, if we have a goal in our life or we have a lot of things to do, then it will run fast leaving us not enough time and sometimes in vice versa. I also started feeling the same way when days passed and everything in my life becomes so routine. It started feeling like life is too boring and nothing much to do. There was not a single thing that keeps me motivated and my longing love for Ishana has made me so exhausted.

I always thought of doing something big but I was at a breakeven point where I was blank like white paper and pen was not in my hands. Even though I wish to do something, my mind pulls me back.

One day suddenly Ferranti messaged me and said "Bruh! We are going to be graduated soon from our school and your Ishana got admission to a university in the US. So, she will be leaving India!"- That was a great shock for me!

I am doing my studies in Kerala and I can't even travel to Mumbai for finding her. Now she is getting ready for her studies in US that made zero hope for me to meet her again. There is no point in telling the issues anymore. I can't live without her and if I started longing for her again, I would burn my half-life in tension and stress. So, without getting an idea, how can I calm this god-forsaken mind of me.

I messaged Ferranti "hey! Bruh, can you please tell me all the details regarding which college and course she is going to take".

He promised to give me all the information, he would get! but I have no idea what to do with that information. So, for the first and last time! I thought of giving a message to her on Facebook to make her understand what I am going through and anyways, what should I need to fear now? everything will be going to get ruined soon. So, it was like a do-or-die situation for me. If she goes to the US, it will be very difficult for me to find her or impress her. Even if I try with whatever means I have.

I took her Facebook account and opened the message bar. I started typing everything from the beginning! from the day of my dreams with the hope she will also get a spark of something in her heart. I strongly believed; she would understand me. My message went on like an essay and I couldn't even stop at a point. I want to talk to her a lot, that I always wish to be by her side and listen to her until my last breath. Every single cell in my body will say her name, that much I am involved in her. Love is an amazing feeling always and whenever I started thinking about her all my senses go blind and she was the only thing in this world that I could feel around.

I don't know whether anyone in this world would love someone, this much sincere and with devotion. I dedicated each and every second of my life to her from the first day she comes into my life. All my dreams, ambitions, and passions are aligned with her and without her in the first place, I would have been in somewhere else without even having a dream or passion.

After sending the message, I eagerly waited for her to see what all I have in my mind. Minutes and hours feel like decades and I got tensed each second. "how she is going to feel about me and what she is going to reply!"- I got tensed.

I waited for 5 hours and I couldn't take it anymore. So, I message Ferranti about this "Bro I messaged her, but she is not replying?"

After few minutes, Ferranti viewed my message and he asked "What did you message her?".

"Everything bro! I messaged her everything I ever wanted to tell her. What I feel about her and whatever I have done for her and everything that happened in my life, the coincidences, the day I saw her for the first time and all."- I said

"You have done a big mistake; she is going to block you without even reading your message. You could have waited a little more to find some other better time to start a conversation, then she would have at least listened to you."- he said

I had already sent the message and now I can't take it back! I got tensed hearing what he said. If she blocks me now, I can't even talk to her again. I don't understand why my life is like this, she is my soul and life but I was just a stranger to her till now.

"Bro, can you do anything about this?"- I asked him, with a hope that he could do something!

"No, bruh! I am helpless in this. She is a very stubborn girl, if she took a decision then that will be final."- he said

Pleading or getting emotional to him is not going to make any change in the sense. He helped me a lot now itself without seeking anything from me. I wondered how a stranger like him came into my life and help me like this to open many doors of mystery that was in front of me, Now I know her character, her likes, dislikes, and many more. I don't know how to thank him for all this because in our life, we can't just give a 'thank you' for things beyond valuable.

"It's okay bro, let her do what she likes and whatever happens is my fate, what else can I say."- I said to him.

"You are a unique personality bruh! I don't understand you always. It's really weird sometimes, can anyone love someone so deep, without even knowing what the other person's feelings are?" – he said

"Even I know, I am weird about this but being stupid in love is the basic formulae for being truthful, isn't it? If I started doubting in my love, then what's the value of it?"- I said.

"But bruh! She is going to leave India soon and I don't know how you are going to make this?"- he told

Just like how curious he is, I also doubted that!

"I don't know bro! As long as she is not committed, I will try my luck."- I said.

"What if she gets committed with someone else before you?"- he asked curiously!

"I will live the rest of my life, with her sweet memories! But I don't know, How I am going to live without her!"- I said with a little pain in my heart.

"I don't know what to tell you, but let me give you an advice "Don't trust anybody and don't believe in this kind of love and ruin your life."- he said.

He started talking like my elder brother/sister! Whatever. But what all he said will not go into my head, at this moment. I have only one aim and that was "Ishana". Even if I make a million-dollar that doesn't make me happy without her, being on my side.

"I don't know whether I will ruin my life or not in her loss. If I don't get her then I will move on with my life, maybe! but if I get her then all this waiting and pain will be extra happiness, isn't it?"- I asked.

"I don't know bruh! But I know she is really lucky to have someone who loves her this much, I wish I could be her!"- he said.

That sounds weird but as he said, I will do anything to make her feels lucky. Now it has been nearly 8 years that I am loving her without even having many things to strengthen my hope. But I was at the point of not knowing whether she exist or not? To a point that I see her with my own eyes, that itself is a huge hope I want to rely on. I believe, all these don't just come randomly because I never expected any of these things with perfect planning in my mind but most of the time, everything comes to me by itself and that's what makes me stand where I am now.

"mmm"- I replied because I don't know what to tell him other than a gesture.

"Bruh! One of her best friends told me that she is going to join Waterbay University in Connecticut. She is planning to do a course related to public administration there."- he said.

"Thank you so much, bro, I won't forget you ever in my life. You have helped me a lot and also your help gives me a lot of hope and what all things you shared about her, helped me a lot to understand her better."- I said.

"Oh! That means you are telling a bye! Isn't it bruh"- he texted with a laughing smiley!

"Nothing like that bro, after she leaves the school. I won't have anyone to help me with her information, isn't it? When you are telling about her, it used to feel like she was just in front of my eyes."- I said

Many times, when I see her pictures send by Ferranti to me, she will be with her friends or family always and she will be smiling all the time. Always I thought like "how fortunate I will be if I was a student of her class." I would have watched her whole day and enjoy the things she would do in front of me. I have seen her singing, her unexpected clicks, and her videos, in everything she was so happy and it was like an aura always spreading through her head. If she comes to my life as my wife, I am sure that I could achieve anything in this world.

"Anyway, bruh! I am not going to message you anymore. She is my friend too and sharing her information with an unknown guy without her knowledge is not a good thing. Anyway, after knowing your story, I couldn't resist helping you with what I have and now keeping our friendship forward, will make me guilty if she comes to know about this."- he said.

"Sorry! Please don't think like that, I won't do anything that hurts her, and I will never tell anyone about what you have done for me."- I promise.

That was the last time Ferranti messaged me and it was like I again come back into where I was. Now I don't know what she is doing and why she is not messaging me back for what I had sent. Many questions, again started confusing me in my head.

Days passed and as usual, I somehow managed to

distract my mind with the other things in my life. The final year project got started in the 3rd year itself and I also got busy with it. I took mechanical engineering seeing "3 idiots" movie. In that movie, the hero will make a generator that can control voltage and current in whatever way he wants and he has even done a Cesarean delivery which was very complicated by using a sucker and vacuum pump that pulls the head of the baby out. Just because of his brain, he impressed his professor who hates him, who was the father of his girlfriend also and at the end, he became a famous scientist and he gets her girlfriend at the climax.

By seeing all these fantasies, even I wish I could build a space rover that can get me where ever she goes or a Time machine that can give me multiple chances in life, we can't make any of these shits in our college because what we have is a 20-mark brain and 2000 bucks per person which makes 10000 bucks' in total. With that capability! what maximum we could make will be a sweeping machine. At last, we end up doing some computer designs of modified vane pump with the help of cracked design software, which even saved the 10000 bucks that we would have spent if we would have gone for a complex something. As I was in a team of some good students, my workload is also very less. They started doing all the job and I financed their snacks. Things are so easy if there is someone to help and we have some pocket money with us.

Every night before I go to sleep, I used to take my Facebook and check whether she saw my message or not, and in March, I suddenly got her reply. My eyes started getting wet seeing her notification and I got excited and tensed at the same time to know what she has replied, my hands started shivering and my body started getting so hot. Which was like I am going to get a heart attack or some kind of trauma. I slowly calmed my mind and hold all my braveness to open the message.

"Hey! Are you mad? First of all, your language sucks. Your DP looks like you are some kind of slum and you want to love me, isn't it? I don't even know you and how could you even imagine that I would love you seeing all this scrap about you. You know what? I will love a boy of my standards only and what you have? Your shitty love story won't work to impress me. Go and try it with someone else in your slum. One more thing, if you ever try to drag me again like this, I make your bloody ass bleed."- she messaged.

By the time I read this message, she blocked me and went away. I felt like digging the ground and go directly to hell. All these years of waiting and my bloody love, just to hear all these insulting words from her? I couldn't even believe that she was the one who is telling all this to me because She always used to care for me in my dreams and now, in reality, she just called me a slum and she felt like, I am unsuitable for her.

Maybe this is "the first and last day" I will be talking with her, my mind nodded. As she said I am mad or otherwise how could someone love anyone like this for no reason. Even she was looking for a guy who is rich and beautiful like her but when she was in my dreams or when I first saw her in the magazine, I never wish her to be rich or talented like she was in her real life. Even if she was poor, I would love her like a queen because she is always like that in my heart.

My heart broke into pieces after that and It was like a trauma. I took leave and stayed back in my hostel room, crying alone when no one else is there and with passing days my pain gets more and more and I couldn't bear it. Is it my fault to born into a middle-class family? and not having enough wealth like her or being not the boy of her dreams? I started calling god in whatever foul words I could, for writing my life most pathetically. He would have simply avoided doing this to me by not showing her in my dreams. Then I would have lived happily without even having a dream or an ambition. But now I have grown all these dreams in my heart for the past 8 years and not even a single day, I thought of losing her in my mind in some ways and especially not in a way that I encountered now.

14

PAIN AND HARDWORK

After that incident, I got completely down and depressed. I started becoming a chain smoker and I fell for whatever addictions that I could find, to fill the gap that she left in my heart. I was completely addicted to her and her loss made me like a lost soul. I know, no other addictions in this world could make up for the loss I incurred. I got lost in Cigarettes and sometimes even weeds and kinds of stuff. I felt like life is falling apart and no one else could ever put it back. Even I thought of ending this waste life but I was so afraid. I was afraid like always and when I get afraid, my hormones play their job. One day it waked my lost mind too. I was sitting at the top of my hostel smoking weed with my friends and I was telling my story to them. They all laughed saying I was mad, just like them anyone who comes to know my story is going to tell the same. What they are telling is true isn't it that who else in this world would get depressed for loving someone they never get to know each other. Talking about my whole life, the total time that I ever get to see her in real was the few hours during that tournament, and other than that I never even get a single chance to have a conversation with her.

One question was raised by my friend hearing my story! "What if you were rich bro? Do you think she would have accepted your love?". That question just made me think again. I just read what she said only and I never thought about the other possibilities. What if I get rich? If I get rich somehow, will she accept me? She didn't say that I am an ugly guy or she would never love me! She just said, she only loves someone who is of her standards. Why can't I get into her standards and become rich! My energy hormones started raising from nowhere and I plunged the weed cigar under my foot and went from there without giving any proper reply to them.

I juiced my brain on thinking what to do next, every day, and just like usual, I got a clue by itself. This time, it comes as spam mail. It was a message from an MBA college where they highlighted the annual CTC. I got amazed by seeing the salary package of the students, who got placed in the top companies.

I started researching about the best colleges in this world and the companies which come for placement. I understood as the ranking of colleges goes high, placement packages will go high. Then I researched how to get into these colleges. I got the list of entrance examinations and the minimum qualification marks to apply. My researches extend to how to get into any top university, near Ishana's college. But I changed my mind because getting closer to her will make me distracted again. So, I tried to stick with the old plan of getting into the topmost college. The fee structure just shocked me as I can't afford it by myself so my research went on to find scholarships and other helping hands.

This passion makes me sleepless and I started waking at 4'0 clock, whatever be the time I went to sleep. I am not a brilliant student to pass this kind of top-level exams and most colleges consider higher grade points for the toppers in a university and their extracurricular certificates. I also got some extracurricular certificates so that was not an issue but I was a 6 pointer in the CGPA which makes me not even close to the university rankings, in my f**king dreams. My 6th-semester exams were scheduled in a 2-week gap and I decided to score well on that. I took leave for my classes and decided to study by myself.

My head starts paining because of taking an extra

load than my usual schedule, but I never want to quit. I keep on moving until my brain starts cooling by itself and things start getting in my way. I understood one thing that if we are determined for something unusual then in first, our body will react negatively to it and if we keep working on it without a break then they find us undefeatable. That will slowly turn them into positive and make them work along with us to succeed in our life.

Finally, the university exams came and I wrote my exams better than ever and other than usual! I felt so much of fullness in my mind and it feels like I started doing something great in my life.

Just after the 6th-semester exams got over and without giving a semester break our 7th semester starts the next day itself because it was our final year and there is much more workload than before. So, we all started doing our projects and assignments in advance for completing it, within the deadline. I also joined along with my project partners and helped them in designing our project. My change was visible in everything I do. I got more disciplined and energetic. My anger issues get away from me and I started behaving friendly to everybody. Maybe because it's the final year at our college or because I got better in my moods, everyone starts behaving so loving to me.

For the first time, I started involving in the activities of my friends and batchmates. I started telling jokes and weird things along with them. I understood one of my big mistakes that I had lost a lot of fun and cherishing moments along with them. Now it's final year and 75% of our college life are over. I could have changed a little before itself and now it's very late. Life is like this! if we run beyond something and don't see the value of things around, we will regret in the end even if we get or do not get the things we chase for. It's not bad to chase things you love. I was also chasing my love for so long but it was just a part of our life if we keep our eyes wide open and look around! You would find many other things to get happiness, like our family, our siblings, friends, relatives, family functions, parties with friends, vacation trips, delicious foods, the happiness of helping others. Especially the things we have right now like our youngness, energy, that freshness of life, Guts to do anything, and a healthy body. If you chase for something and miss out on the pleasure of enjoying all this, after we achieve our dream then there won't be anything left or the left wouldn't be in the same beauty as it is before.

By understanding that, getting regretful for what I loss won't make anything better, so I decided to enjoy the present and work hard for my future because I don't want to be regretful again for not using the right moment, I got.

I worked harder and smarter for reaching my goals. Slowly all my hard work shows results that I became my class topper for the first time and that was never expected by anyone includes me. That boosted my confidence to work hard. Along with my academics, I focused on GMAT, CAT kind of entrance tests for joining the top universities in the world. I was good at Math always not in the sense of marks but in the sense of understanding so It was a little easy for me to prepare for the entrance examination. I remembered why I studied math very hard for the first time! It was because of her that I know math very well now and even I teased myself for wasting my time in math when I come to know that she is not the one who wrote that article in the magazine. But now it's useful for me in the journey for achieving something great.

When we start working smart or start enjoying what we do, the time will go so fast. It felt like I skipped months in between a 6-month duration of the semester because the University exam date was published and it felt like nothing much I had done in between. Putting back all my preparation aback, I focused on my exams and do it well than ever before.

We started running through December and only 5 more months got left in the college. Everyone started getting emotional and Personally! for me, I am not going to miss anyone but by seeing the emotions of others I understood that I had missed a great life in this college as a student and as a friend, I lost the chance to become a best friend of this amazing guys. In our life, these kinds of losses can't be got back because friendship is all about the memories we share. Even if it's good or bad, the higher the memories higher the bonding will be. That's why some enemies in our school or college become our best friends after graduation. During school time, they may be enemies all the time and in all their thought processes, only that enemy will be coming. But after graduation, all the fights and bad memories they share will become sweet memories or even funny parts to remember in our life, that why we always remember our school or college time enemies or those who irritated us a lot.

In my life, I lost the good memories and the bad memories so probably no one is going to remember me after this college and it's a sure thing.

We finished off our project in January and presentations started. We were the first group to start so, we were the ones who finished off first. After that, classes were rarely scheduled and everyone got busy with workshops and preparing for final exams. I also tried to balance my Entrance preparation along with all my other works.

When our life goes so fast-paced, even if you enjoy it! There won't be any interesting things to talk about. My life also gets into such a stage where if I am writing a book about me then I would be the boring character that you could ever find and certainly that book too.

Every day was very normal and routine in the activities that I do, even I wished something need to happen in my life for a small turn around or for an adventure but what special is going to happen in the life of a guy who is simply sitting in the hostel and attending classes or workshops?

I just thought of getting a twist and twist comes in the form of an allergy. I got affected by a f**king skin disease above all the bloody things that are happening till the time and I was in the middle of all the preparations. That just made me pissed off to god! Again. Whenever life starts going on a good and calm path, something like this kind of hell would break directly into my head. He could have put everything in a single stance and take me into the comma stage directly but who doesn't want entertainment! He was just playing in my life in one way or another. My skin dried out and the blood starts oozing out in some areas. My face started getting dry and black spots started appearing here and there and totally that made me an ugly shit. I consulted a doctor and he named it in some kind of blah blah blah that I couldn't understand. Now the interesting part! Not for me, but for others to see. As medication became a part of my life that just made me look like a fat boy with a bunhead. By the 2 months' time, I nearly gained like 35kg and my total weight becomes 90+. It was just enough for spoiling my total mood when I got weighed.

My 6th-semester result came out in April and I got 9.2 percentile that makes me just 0.4 percentile away from the first rank holder in the university for the 6th-semester. That was a huge relief during all these pains. But the shitty ranks didn't make me happy in the mirrors.

As we are the first batch, no specific companies came to our campus for the placements and getting placed with B. tech! Became just a part of our dreams. I don't have any issues with that as I already made some other plans for myself.

My final year exam date has come and due to the persistence, I put in the studies. Even with all these difficulties I somehow managed to write it well! but I was not at all satisfied. Anyway, thinking about something that is over doesn't make sense to me now.

As the exams are over, I focused completely on my entrance tests. I didn't have enough money to apply for GMAT and some other international level tests. Even I don't want to ask for money from my parents as they had spent almost everything they saved for my higher studies. So, I decided to do some part-time jobs and make some money. Due to the medication, I even looked like a mid-30's man that made me look like a professor. I started teaching engineering students of my age and even above for their supplementary exams. I started teaching them a full textbook in 4 days by splitting it into 4 modules and that takes one module a day. As it is the supplementary exam, they also don't want to lag the subject with unnecessary topics. When this kind of task comes to your life then you will understand that you can learn everything very faster than you ever expect. I never used to study things this faster and when it comes to a profession, nothing just stopped me from doing it. I was never a fast learner nor the last day learner but my life teaches me how to live through whatever the situation is!

Finally, with all the money I earned from the different places, I applied to all the exams on my list. The results of my students came out and they also got passed with some good marks. They shared their happiness through phone calls and messages and I was on cloud 11 to this much gratitude in my life. I was not a good teacher who had an abundance of knowledge but I just had the knowledge of how to pass the exams with minimum marks and that's what I had shared with my students also. I just told them whatever I felt necessary and yah! The results come out with whatever I had wished to happen. After this success, all the institutes that I teach before offered me good pay for teaching their students.

I also promised them that I will take the classes till I will be here not because they offered me good pay but because I felt so good seeing other's happiness in their eyes after they cleared the worst obstacle in their life. Even if I played a small role in their struggles, their results felt like mine too. That's the time I understood the value of other's happiness in my mind.

My exams also came one by one and by November 2017, I finished off all the exams and waited eagerly for my results. By the time, I again started working out in the gym and controlled my diets but like before!

it doesn't give me any good results. My skin slowly started recovering but black spots persist in my face and body and that makes me wear a full sleeve shirt and a lousy jean always.

After few days of attending the GMAT exam, the scorecard got out and with a lot of curiosity and hope, I checked my result. I scored 742 marks on the GMAT and that just made me eligible for any top universities in the world. Even after getting this huge success, I didn't feel anything like I always do and that just made me confused "I don't know what happened?" anyway it's the worst thing that anyone could come through after a big success. My happiness hormone may not have work, I guess! because I used to get over-excited and happy for even a small thing in my life and now everything that I could ever seek is in my hands but I am not feeling anything not even close to happiness. I told about my score on GMAT to everyone who loves me. They also started showing their happiness and regards but I don't know what I am going to do after getting a seat in some top university! Why should I become rich? Do I get happy for becoming rich? I don't know! Maybe the time needs to show by itself.

In this kind of situation that I normally used to think about my fantasies. If I would have a time machine in my hand, I could have simply gone to the future and check whether I am happy or not and would change my decisions accordingly. Even though it was practically not possible, I always wished to have one. Anyway, just leave it!

So, what just happened in my life is that, if we ever dream of getting something in our life then it will start feeling so big and glittery. But if it comes to us in real, then its value will fade away by itself! Especially when we work for something that doesn't align with our call of destiny. Maybe the thing I just achieved was like that and that may be the reason I couldn't find any happiness in that. But after deep thinking, I decided to apply to all the top universities and made my mind, saying "Let's see where I will end up".

I got a 90% scholarship from many places and I got admitted to the most prestigious university in London. My life started looking very fascinating for the outside people. My life journey was so fascinating too that I was never a top-class student or a brilliant mind but my love for Ishana just takes me to the paces that I never even thought of in my weirdest dreams. Everyone conveyed their wishes and regards for me and many people who got to hear my news, called me from nowhere and congrats me. The hard part is that I don't feel any kind of excitement about what I have achieved or what I could have achieved after this. This is the worst thing that could happen to anyone but that just made me grounded from going to some kind of cloud 11 again.

15

THE TURNING POINT

It was the first time I am going somewhere far away from my home town so, I started missing everyone and everything from the moment I reached London. Only a few Indians were there in my college so clearly, I felt so being foreign there. Students from different ethnicities and cultures make the campus looks different and there was a kind of new vibe there. After few induction sections, I started interacting with everybody, and what I think about the whites started falling apart. I thought whites were so arrogant and rude. When I send the friend request to Ishana's schoolmates, whites were the ones who act so rude in their messages.

I got a few good friends also and three of my best friends were David, Evelyn, and Rosey. David and Evelyn were also cousins and they were from Connecticut which makes me remember Ishana as she was studying there somewhere. Rosey was from London itself and she was our tour guide, whenever we go outside. When we get so close, I told them my complete story and my lost love 'Ishana'. They don't mock me as everyone else does but they consoled me for whatever happened. After that, they started doing something to always engage me from getting over the depression of my old memories.

I also started forgetting about Ishana in their company and my college life started getting interesting. I opened up my eyes and see the new world around me, I was in a place full of aspiring people. I started wondering, how I get here because from most of the people's stories I understood they were so brilliant, and getting into a college like this was their sole dream. Even my friends were such kind of a people who worked their whole life to reach here. They were so enthusiastic and excited to become a part of the legacy that the college shared with the topmost leaders in this world. I also started getting proud day by day and also started my competition for survival. Everyone there was in a race to succeed and whoever lags will be out of the race so I also tried to be the fittest among the survivors.

Our work schedule was so tight like work and extracurriculars go hand in hand. Every day was so exciting and interesting, at the same time very hectic too as the workload was so heavy. Evelyn was a very brilliant girl, she used to help me whenever I asked for and even started helping me without even asking. She started understanding all my likes, dislikes, and weak points. So, I also started enjoying her company.

I used to call her a barbie with the soda glass. She is very beautiful like a barbie doll and she has a power glass that covers half of her face. She is so funny and a lively person, moreover she loves my India. She always used to tell stories of her experience when she went to India. Even though many Indians were in that college, she seems more Indian to me.

David and Rosey get committed within a few months and they became so busy in their romance. Evelyn was a studious girl she was not interested in love and all, so we used to study together always. We started spending our time together from the study hours we share to the rest of the time, till we go to sleep. She always hangs out with me and I also don't have any other special ones to hang around. We used to sit along in all our lectures and even if she or I get sick also, we became so upset and moody. I even felt like we were in a relationship but I don't know whether I have a feeling like that to her because still deep inside my heart, it tells the name of Ishana only.

One year just passed that way and our first result came out. I and Evelyn got a twin score which makes us the 5th rank from the university. David and Rosey were distracted in their studies due to their romance, I guessed! because their grade points were not up to their standards but still not that bad too.

David and Rosey asked for a party from us. So, we decided to go for an outing. Rosey has an own mini cooper on campus so going somewhere is not much of a difficulty. So, we went to a pub and had some drinks and shared each and every small moment we shared together on campus. There was nothing crazy we had done still we enjoyed a lot living on campus. After the drinks, Rosey put an idea of going to a film. David and Rosey were in a dating mood so they take us to the "Paradise cinemas" in London! We can't find theaters like this in Kerala, it was very beautiful which looks like a Royal hall. The movie which was running in that theater was "Falling in love", which seems like a romantic movie on the poster and David took the tickets for us.

When we find our seats, it was pretty dramatic. A cushioned seat with a small table lamp in the side where people need to sit in couples, David and Rosey were all set to start their romancing. I got tensed seeing others around, it was like a perfect place for dating and everyone seems like lovers too. David and Rosey started their romance also. They were like they don't want to watch the movie but just need to do what they do every day, their romance.

The movie starts, Me and Evelyn were the only ones who were watching the movie and others started kissing, hugging, caring, what else! We also started getting irritated, sitting in the middle of a romance hub. The hero and heroine were looking into the sea and talking about their feelings, laying on the grass bed beside the shore. Suddenly she kissed him and said, "wasn't expecting that?". I looked at Evelyn and she was already looking at me. "Do you want to kiss?"- she asked. I got shocked and silent for a second and keep staring at her with an expression of half no, I don't know! Suddenly she comes so near to me and we started kissing. It was my first kiss; many things go in my head while kissing her but she just slowly touched my head and scroll her hands through my head. It was like, all my stress and pain went away in a second and I couldn't restrict myself from doing that also.

After a long kiss, we settled back and looked at each other in shock. We had done something we never expected. The girl in the movie asked about "expecting it" and yah "it was never expected". We didn't talk anything after that and as David and Rosey were sitting in front of us, they won't have seen what we have done too, that was the only relief!

We went for dinner after that and David, Rosey! They found out that something is happening between us because we were not looking at each other.

By seeing my embarrassment, David asked: "Dude, what happened to you guys suddenly? Why are you even not looking at each other?"

I got tensed in that question. How can I say, I kissed his cousin! "No! No, Nothing. Nothing happened"- I started hiccups with my words.

Evelyn also kept silent.

Suddenly David said, "Hey Dude, you kissed Eve?".

I shocked! How did he find that? "What! What are you saying?"- I asked in a tensed voice.

"I know dude, when did you start putting lipstick on?."- he tells that and started laughing on Rosey's shoulder.

I became speechless, anyway, they caught us red-handed and what else to lie.

"Hey, don't say this to anyone! It just happened by mistake."- I said.

Evelyn keeps her silence and puts an innocent look on her face. Her eyes started sparkling through her soda glasses filled with tears which makes her look like the cat Gif that we usually see on Facebook!

Anyway, I just patted her head and slowly tried to divert the topic with other matters like upcoming placements and all.

That day was just amazing and I never enjoyed this much in my entire life and even I forget about everything that had ever happen in my life.

After dinner, we get into our rooms so late. So, I directly fell asleep without even removing my shoes.

The next day morning, Evelyn put a message that she is sick and she is not coming today. I got tensed about her! "Are you okay? Do you want to go to the hospital?"- I enquired.

"It's okay, I will be fine after a small sleep."- she said.

"Oh okay! Then I am also not going anywhere. I will stay in my room itself and if you feel anything bad, just call me. I will come there"- I said.

After few hours she texted me and asked me to come to her room. "In a minute"- I replied and rush to her room.

She was laying in her bed with bed sheets on and I asked her "How you feeling? Is everything okay?".

"I don't know! I am not feeling well"- she said.

"Okay get up, let's go to a hospital"- I removed her bed sheet and hold her up.

"NO! no, I don't want to go to the hospital."- she said.

"Why? Do you have any other problems?"- I asked.

"I am not feeling well, I just don't know why!" – she said.

I understood that there is something in her mind.

"what happened! Tell me, we can fix it."- I said.

"Nothing! Just leave it."- she said.

I started getting an intuition like she is telling something related to what had happened yesterday.

"Do you have any problem with me?"- I asked?

"No! why should I have any problem with you?"- she said.

"Then what, tell me openly! We can fix it."- I said.

She started getting tensed and her face starts sweating and I can feel that she wants to tell me something. I sit beside her in the bed and hugged her and said "Tell me, whatever your problem is? I will be with you!"

"I hope you understand me! I didn't kiss you by mistake yesterday"- she said.

"What do you mean?"- I asked, curiously.

"It doesn't mean anything! I just love you. I know you have a dream girl and you can't see me like that. It's okay we can just be friends."- she said with her eyes filled in tear.

I don't know what happened to me at that time. I couldn't find Ishana more than Eve's friendship because even after knowing my love to Ishana, she loved me and even cared for me a lot even when I was depressed and diseased and I know that in the future too she will care for me more than anyone else in this world.

"You know what! I hate you"- I said.

She got shocked and look at me with a weird face and it's funny when she gives that look. I am just loving all her weird mannerisms and her care for me so how can just reject her. Hurting Eve, for a girl who called me a slum doesn't make any sense for me that time. So, I decided to become a 'gem' for someone who values me rather than becoming a stone for someone, I don't deserve.

"Yes! I hate you for thinking like that because I love you too, maybe more than you!"- I said.

She started crying and laughing at the same time and get from her bed and jumped into me with a huge hug and for the first time in my life, I understood how it feels! When two people, love each other.

I didn't get it! How she fell in love with a guy like me. She was very fit and looking so adorable but me, I am like 85Kg balloon structured guy and not looking so handsome with a lot of ugly spots on my face and all over my body. With the knowledge of my complete past and seeing all these not beautiful kinds of stuff, she loves me, and that what makes her so special to me.

After that, we had written a beautiful love story about our life. We started making the most romantic day and night that one could ever think of! One year just passed like heaven and she makes me completely live in her world. In this one year, I never thought about Ishana or anything that bothered me in my past.

Placement season has come and I got placed in an Investment banking company as an Associate Manager in Mumbai. Evelyn also started looking for an organization that could place her in India itself so that we could stay together. Finally, she also got placed in one of the big Multinational companies in Mumbai itself as a Digital Accounts specialist. That job was not up to the mark for her talents and her rank but she just chooses that job to be with me by simply rejecting all other big offers that came into her hand. This mentality of her teaches me that it is not necessary to sacrifice our beloved things for something looking very big. After all, we put the standards for valuing things and 'Eve' put higher value for me than anything else.

These two years of life at my college in London give me a lot in academics, some shared values from bigger minds, and an awesome job with a highly appreciated salary package. More than everything else, my college life gives me Evelyn.

Evelyn was something very special because I never thought I would have committed with her and the most amazing thing I could ever become is that I was her first lover. She doesn't stay single because she was loving some dream boy as I do. But all her dreams were in her studies and she was a kind of bookish girl which makes her hide from all the handsome boys outside.

Our 2-year college life has come to an end and there was not any dramatic emotional scene on my graduation day because everyone was very practical in their life.

David and Rosey got placed in top firms in London and they were happy about their life. They wished us a very beautiful life ahead and we wished them the same. David and Rosey were just my best friends but they are going to my family too after I get married to Eve and also that was the best part in our friendship story.

The other special thing about our graduation day is that it's the day, I am going to meet her parents for the first time. She already introduced me to her parents through phone calls but I was a little bit nervous to meet them in real.

She was a little fast about all these things but in my case, I didn't even talk to my parents regarding this. I don't know how they are going to react on hearing this. They would have never expected their boy to get married to a foreign girl. Now also I intentionally avoided them from my graduation day because I needed some more time to present this topic in front of them.

My English was a little funny because of my Indian accent and my limited vocabulary. That makes me a little unconfident to present myself in front of her parents but somehow, I put up a confident face and went to meet them. Her parents were waiting for us in the graduation hall and when they saw us, they stood up and come near to us with a wide smiling face.

Evelyn's mom was just like her, very beautiful and adorable. Her dad is 6 feet 2-inch-tall guy with a wide chest and well build body, which makes him far handsome than I could ever imagine becoming, that also he is in his 60's.

I come to know his age because the day before graduation was his birthday and I saw Evelyn wishing him a happy 62nd birthday. Otherwise, he is not looking like the '60s, not even more than 50. He is just that handsome, looking like Hugh jackman in the movie "Scoop", even I envy him!

My relationship with Evelyn not just cured my broken heart but cured my physical body also. She was the motivation behind me getting back into my regular shape and even my skin started curing faster and my face turned better than ever. Love is a miracle and if someone cares about you so much and you understand the value of it, everything in your life will turn beautiful.

Her dad welcomed me with a hug and greet me with "Namaste". "Hello, Uncle"- I replied. Usually, we call all elders as "Uncle" in India but I was not sure about here. I just tried my luck and Most of the foreigners are thinking like we Indians greet by "Namaste". But in my life, I never greeted anyone with that and even Namaste feels like a foreign word to me either. In Kerala, it is called "Namaskaram" and it is too lengthy to substitute a simple word like hi or hello.

"So, when are you inviting us to India?"- he asked.

"Very soon Uncle, I will make all the arrangements and I will call you. Both of you should come to my home."- I said

Her mother was just like her. She didn't talk to me much but kept a beautiful smile all the time.

I could get the feeling that they are respecting Indians a lot and how they keep relationships in their life.

Her dad started talking about India and the last time they visited India and now I got where she gets the talent of explaining things. She also once explained her experience in India and it was an exact mimic of how her dad is explaining.

While talking with her parents, I understood some things that she never mentioned before. Her dad has an own business in automobiles, they own a Porsche showroom in the US and he was doing business in the stock market also which simply makes him a millionaire. Her mother is a doctor and she has a 1200+ bed hospital in the central city, which was her family-owned business that also worth millions probably. All of them in their family were highly reputed in one or another way and that just makes me felt like a tiny poop in front of them.

My eyes started bulging out hearing all this. She never told me that she was this rich and what special about this is that she is their only daughter which makes her a billionaire already. She was so simple all the time and someone not even mistakenly would expect that she is this rich. I thought millionaires would look like something else and now what I am seeing is some normal people in plain dresses. How can these people be so simple as this! I wonder?

After hearing all their part, I told them about my financial status and the way I got raised. I asked them not to expect too much when they come to India because I don't want to get insulted when they visit my home or my village. She grabbed my hand hearing this, in front of them, and looked at her parents with her innocent cat pose.

They also started smiling and their approach just flabbergasting. They are not even looking at what I am in past or my financial status. What they were looking forward to is that "whether I would keep their daughter happy or not". I thought only Indian parents would think like this and act so family-minded. All my imaginations about foreigners were wrong, I thought the foreign parents wouldn't even care about discussing their daughter's future with his boyfriend. They seemed to me like a white Indian, especially a south Indian parent who is very conservative about taking decisions wisely.

I liked her whole family and I just wondered! Do I deserve them? Because they are such perfect! and in my life, I never expect not even half close to this. I felt so much gratitude in my heart.

They started announcing the results and we settle back to our seats. They started calling rank holders from 10th to 1st. They called my name in the 4th and it was like a great honor receiving a rank from the most prestigious universities in the world and that also in front of my Girlfriend's family. I walked proudly to my 'Eve' and she hugged me and kiss me on my cheek and that also felt like another honor for making my girlfriend proud.

They called 3rd and 2nd rank holders and for the remaining person, everyone put their eyes sharp to know who is going to be that prestigious gold medalist in the topmost university in the world. Breaking the curiosity of everyone, they called "Evelyn" to the stage and it was really unexpected because after we get committed her focus was completely on me and in most of our study hours also she used to waste her time by simply looking at me but I got really happy and proud to see my girlfriend achieved the most glittery position in our university.

That day was full of surprises to me, it was like a dream day. She jumped with excitement and run to the stage. They gave the microphone to her and she started thanking everybody from her childhood including her parents and dedicated her medal to me. I started crying because of that happiness, that's the first time in my life I couldn't bear happiness.

She ran to me after that and put her medal in my

neck and said "It's because of you that I achieved this. You are the one who always makes me feel so special and I want to share all my success just with you, now and forever."- While hugging her I felt like the whole world, I was holding in my hands.

16

THE BOOMERANG

After the graduation day, I went back to Kerala and she goes to her hometown in Connecticut. Due to the corona pandemic, our countries got closed and we also got stuck in our places. I started missing her so badly and we were supposed to join our companies in August and October. That put us in a very big struggle to pass each day since March.

Talking through the video calls doesn't make anything better than putting fire to the already burning loneliness. The most irritating thing was the time gap, when it was night there then it will be morning here and vice versa.

One day, I busted the topic of Evelyn to my parents and they got shocked first that they never imagined a picture of me with a white American girl. We used to call a foreigner "Sayippu for male and Madhama for female." I also kept it a secret because my friends are going to tease me by saying that I am going to marry a Madhama. It was not a bad thing but still seems weird as it is very rare.

I put her in the skype call and started introducing her to my parents and friends. She also tried to speak with them in her broken "Malayalam" that I teach her while we were bored or get tired of romancing. Everyone just loved her because she was very polite and beautiful. Even they said, "If her hair is a little blacker, she would have also looked like an Indian girl". That was true! Even though she is an American, many times even I felt her like an Indian girl. She always has special grace on her face and smile, more than that her culture was very similar to our Indians and her ethics are even much better than mine.

If I started talking about her good qualities, I can't stop it in simple words. She was just full of surprises and great qualities. Sometimes I even felt not good enough for her but she never made me felt like that. She always respected me in a certain way that she always tried to put me at the top of everything when a conversation comes. I don't think that any girl would do this for her boyfriend in this 21st century.

Somehow, we managed two more months romancing through the phone and I got the date for joining my company. I got suited up and packed up everything for relocating to Mumbai for joining my first job after all the struggles.

I took a 2 BHK apartment for rent in Bandra with planning that Evelyn could also stay with me when she comes to join here and I also got a car, provided by the company.

The first few days were an induction program and I will be assisting certain higher-level employees for the next 3 months. I got the chance to closely work with every top-level employee in that firm. Our managing director was a great man and what special about him is he was an alumnus of our college in London. He became my mentor and by seeing my data analysis skills, he even assisted me before submitting his reports. I started feeling how fortunate I am to work for such a reputed company and being treated so well by its managers. Getting a great boss is the luckiest part of a company because they are the ones who make us feel good about the work and sometimes worse about it. For me, I got the best manager and what else, one would need.

Above all this happiness, I was waiting for the day Evelyn comes to Mumbai so that I could see her gain. It has been a huge missing for all these months and Suddenly one day Evelyn got bad news for me that due to corona, her joining date gets delayed till everything starts getting normal. That was a piece of really bad news for us but she was ready to come to India for me as we had already waited so long But I felt like it's better to be where she is now because, in India, COVID-19 was spreading so vigorously that it passed the stage of being controlled by social distancing. Somehow, we consoled each other by understanding the situation.

One Sunday, when I was just simply lying in my bed and thinking about how fortunate I am! All of a sudden, the memory of "Ishana" came into my mind. It's because of her that I had done all this and actually without her, I wouldn't have achieved all this! It has been a long time, I even thought about her and I just wonder, where she will be now and what she will be doing. I am not regretful for what I had done, because Evelyn is also an amazing girl and not less than Ishana in any way. But I will be happy if I would see her one last time so that I could tell her what I achieved.

I had deleted my Facebook that day itself when she messaged me back for the first and last time. Now there is no other way, I could search for her. Maybe because of the nostalgic feel that created in me, I thought of visiting that boxing club that I first saw her, some training was going on there but they permitted me to enter the club and I get inside the ring and look into the seat where she sits and shouts at me that day.

It was a great feeling when we become something and look back into the days, we were nothing. I leave the club with a heart full of unknown emotions and I went to the star bucks that I visited last time, just to taste the costly coffee that is not at all costly anymore. Now I can afford anything I want and I can enjoy all the luxury of being rich but the only loss is the goal I set which makes me what I am today was not there.

I ordered the same expresso shot and sit alone in a chair thinking about what was my feeling when I come here last time.

"Hey, bruh! Is that you?"- someone shouted at me.

I raised my head and look at him because he was shouting just in front of me. Too close that I couldn't see the face first!

It was none other than Ferranti! I was surprised by seeing him.

"Hey, Ferranti! Is this you?"- I asked while giving him a handshake.

"ha-ha! Yes lol"- he said

"You have changed a lot bro; you look so manly! I like your beard"- I said.

"Thank you! By the way, how is your Ishana?"- he asked.

"Are you mocking me? How did I know!"- I asked him!

"What! are you serious bruh? That day, I told her everything about your love and what all you had told me. She also gets impressed with you and told like she is going to contact you afterward."- he said.

Hearing this I got blank for a minute! I couldn't believe my ears.

"But bro, she teased me like a shit that day and even she called me a slum"- I asked in confusion.

"OMG! Bruh, it was not her. It was her cousin Rayan. The same guy whom you beat in the tournament"- he said.

"But how! What? and Why he should do that?"- I asked, my eyes started getting red and my head started feeling so heavy hearing all this.

"I am very sorry bruh! I was cheating you. I first send you a friend request just because Rayan said, I thought of helping him because he got beaten by you in the tournament and he wants to revenge on you."- he said.

"But! How can you, I don't know what to say! She was my life and I could have her love but now it's very late and not going to happen"- I said and started getting very emotional. I controlled my tears and emotions inside my handkerchief.

"Why are you telling me all this after everything is over, I already had moved on with my past"- I asked in a low voice.

"I was cheating you but after hearing your story I tried to help you with whatever I had."- he said.

"So, is that your sympathy for me, what makes you tell her the truth?"- I asked.

"No bruh! I also got cheated in the same like you and then only I understood how painful it was."- he said.

"You got cheated for what?"- I asked.

"I first saw you when my boyfriend was scrolling through my Facebook profile as usual after our romantic hours. He is none other than Rayan itself. He said, you are the one who beats him in the tournament, and by seeing all the mutual friends in your profile, we understood you have something going on in our school. Then I talked with you on an intention to trick you but after hearing your story I got emotional that's why I didn't play any trick with you. Rayan told me to stop talking with you when he felt that I am not good for any use! But I tried to give you all the information about her that I know by that time."- he said.

"But why did he cheat you? Did he come to know that, you helped me?"- I asked.

"By mistake, I told him about your message to Ishana and he tricked Ishana and took her phone and replied to you and after that he, deleted the message itself."- he said.

Now It makes sense but still, I have some more doubts!

"Still, I didn't get, why he cheated you and how?"- I asked in a little more anger because he is not giving a real clarity of what had happened.

"Rayan was loving Ishana too and he asked me to f**koff after he felt no use of me. In that anger, I went to Ishana and told her what Rayan has done"- he said.

Now it makes sense but what the purpose of knowing this now. I bite my teeth because I couldn't suppress my anger. If it was not a public place, I would have at least shout at him just to make my mind calm.

"You could have at least told me about this, that time. Isn't it?"- I asked

"This is a week after I messaged you the last time

and I even tried to contact you on Facebook. But I couldn't find your profile. As Ishana also don't ask me anything after that I thought you guys have talked to each other."- he said.

It was my mistake too that I deleted my Facebook account on emotions. Otherwise, I would have at least come to know all this before itself. I thought that was the worst day in my life but knowing this after all these years, was pretty useless. Now I have a GF and I don't even know where is Ishana. It was like all my dreams come true but I don't have enough hands to hold them. The thing that I wish to achieve all these years would have been mine but what should I do now.

I went to my room and try to sleep for a while because it was an exhausting day for me. I wish I could forget everything after sleep.

When I wake up, I saw 8 missed calls from Evelyn. It was midnight! Oh shit, I forget to call her the whole day and she must be so tensed now. While I was thinking to call back, she again called.

I took the call and she was really tensed in her voice. "I am very sorry Dear; I was a little dizzy so I went to sleep in the afternoon itself."- I cleared my part.

She teased me for a while for making her scared. As I was alone in the apartment, she felt like someone would have kidnapped me or even hurt me. In the case of me, she always acts like my mother.

"I have good news for you."- she said.

"Do you received the joining date?"- I asked, curiously.

"Hey! How did you know!"- she said in surprise.

"What else is happy for me other than you coming to me, dear."- I said.

"OOH! That's so sweet and I have a surprise for you!"- she said.

"What surprise, is your parents also coming?"- I asked with a smile.

"No! A surprise is a surprise. You will get it when I come. I will be coming on November 27th"- she said

This good news was just more than enough, for me to help forget the sadness I have in my heart now. I waited for the day to meet her and like a school kid who counts days for the school tour to come, I also started counting hours and days for her arrival.

17

THE LAST CHAPTER

The day I was waiting to come, November 27th has come and she will be coming on the morning flight so I was eagerly waiting for her arrival.

I told her; I would wait for her at the Airport but she insisted saying that I should prepare her lunch. So, from the morning itself, I started cooking her favorite dishes. she loves Indian butter chicken masala and sushi. Even though I don't like this combination, I would love to make it for her.

I prepared some Kerala dishes along with some western fusions that once I tried experimenting while I was in London. You know what? If you knowing cooking while you were in college, you can become a star. People love to taste good food and I always believe; our culture lies in the taste of our food. If you even look at India itself, in different states, they have different food items, and even how they mix spices in their food shows their character sometimes. For example, Telangana people eat too much chilly/spice and they look rough and tough sometimes but polite in their manners, Tamil Nadu people eat spicily and even add a lot of salt to it, which makes them feels rough and tough outside but very loving inside and Keralites eat less spicy/chilly and used to eat sweeter which makes them looks very sweet outside. It is very generic and nothing to do with the characters of people.

I was not a fast cook so the work I started from the morning 8'0 clock just finished off by 1:00 pm. Her flight will be arriving at 1:20 pm and I eagerly waited for her call. At sharp 1:25 pm, she called me "Darling! I reached the airport. I will come to your apartment directly."

"Come fast! I and my experiments are waiting for you dear."- I said with a smile.

I am super excited to see her after a long time. I already bought her a 'ring' and due to corona and outside issues, I can't plan for a dramatic proposal. So, I decided to make it simple in my apartment. I arranged all the dishes on the dining table and hide the cake I bought for her as today is her birthday too.

My doorbells ring and I ran to open the door. She was standing just in front of me and I stood there for a second and hold her to my chest. It has been so long that I felt her heartbeat and her warmth, it was like I got relief from whatever stress I had till that time. I look forward to a kiss and she stopped in the middle saying "I have a surprise for you."

"First kiss, then surprise."- I told with a smile.

"No! you will be shocked to see this surprise."- she said.

"Okay! Give it, let me see."- I said in curiosity.

"Close your eyes and open only when I say."- she said and closed my eyes with her hands.

"Now open."- she said

It must be a pet or something I guessed because I used to tell her that I love dogs and want to get one when we get a house together. But what I saw just made me so unreal! I couldn't believe my eyes. It was "Ishana", standing in front of me. So real and original but I didn't even know what kind of emotion I was feeling at that moment.

I looked at Evelyn in shock.

"Do you like my surprise?"- she asked.

I couldn't answer that because it's really happy to see her again but seeing her at the wrong time was suffocating for me.

"You have talked about her more than 1000 times when we first became friends and I know how much you love her. Now she is just in front of you and you have all the time in this world to talk with her."- she said with a smile, but I could see the pain in her eyes. I didn't understand why she is doing this now.

"Where did you find her?"- I asked in a low voice.

I felt so awkward talking with her in front of Ishana. She was also standing there staring at us that what we are talking.

"I just searched for her on Facebook one day and come to know that she was in my hometown so I just put her a message and after hearing your name, she asked me to meet her and rest is here."- Evelyn said.

"It's okay! But why did you take her to my apartment? What you are trying to do?"- I asked.

"You love Ishana more than me and I even know that you can't see me in the same way as you are seeing her."- she said and, in her words, I could feel the pain of something unexplainable.

Even if I try to lie, it was true actually still now Ishana has a big place in my heart but still, Evelyn could conquer my emotions over Ishana somehow maybe because I thought, I am not going to get Ishana anymore. But now Ishana is in front of me and ready to hear what all I want to say! And at that moment, I got confused about what to say or even become speechless to resist what all Eve has told.

Cutting through my silence, she asked us to go to my bedroom and talk for some time. She takes me to my room and asked me to stay there and created a space for us to talk.

Whatever the situation is! I don't know what is happening and what is right or wrong? I stood silent with a confused mind, what to do?

"Are you okay!"- Ishana asked.

That's the first time, she is talking to me in real.

She was just in front of me but I felt like I was so far from her.

"I am feeling good, what about you?"- I asked while putting my head down.

"I am great, at last, I got the chance to meet you."- she said.

She is telling what I mean to tell and I don't even know what to tell next so I nodded "MMM"

"I am very sorry, that day it was my cousin who messaged you and I tried to contact you many times after that but I couldn't find any of your information."- she said.

She looks so sorry about what had happened and it was the first time I saw her with a sad face. I always see her smiling even if it's in the pic or dreams. Now seeing her sad just puts me in a huge disgrace. It was because of me that now we are standing like this! In regret.

"It's okay! I had forgotten it there itself."- I said, a lie!

"Good! Is Evelyn your girlfriend?"- she asked.

"Yes, she is my girlfriend."- I said with a slight pain in my heart because I never expected to tell Ishana with my mouth that I have another girlfriend.

"Great! Both of you guys are so lovely."- she said and I saw the same unexplainable pain in her that I had seen in Eve's eyes too.

I didn't understand what is happening here and what I need to do.

"Do you have a boyfriend?"- I asked, That's the first time I prayed to hear from her that she had a boyfriend.

"No, I am still single."- she said with her eyes full of the tear.

I don't know why her eyes get wet like this. I always pray to God for making her feel the same way I feel about her and from her appearance and behavior I am seeing the same me when I was loving her.

I want to wipe her tears, hug her and say I had loved you a lot and still I love you in the same way but now I am standing in the middle of somewhere I can't come back.

She comes near me and give me a tight hug! that I couldn't resist because I saw the same pain, I felt! when I get the message from her "calling me a slum and an unsuitable guy".

Holding her close to my heart I asked Ishana- "Can I ask you something?"

"yes"- she replied.

"Do you love me? Or are you trying to show the empathy for all the struggles I have gone through, for you"- I asked

"I don't know! The way you loved me! That no one would ever do for any girl and also no one ever loved me in the same way you do. Maybe not even close to what you have done. I was not like you were thinking, I was always alone and depressed by the fake people around"- she said and her tears started coming out.

I swiped her tears with my hands. "Please don't cry! In my dreams, you always used to smile and I don't want to see you like this."- I said.

She wiped her eyes and put a smile on her face.

She under my arms, me swiping her tears and Whatever the situation is! That I want to put a smile on her face always. This is all I ever needed and now I have the opportunity to choose what I need for my life. I felt like holding her under my arms till my death and give her all the happiness in this world.

I simply looked at her for a while because I don't know whether she would be in my life anymore! For a moment I wished, I could get her as a friend at least. But doesn't what god plan for us?

I asked her "Now why did you come here?".

"I was searching for you all these years with a hope that someday, you would message me but you didn't! At first, I searched you for curiosity but later my mind started feeling like 'I never want to miss a guy who loves me more than anything in this world' and that's the reason I stayed single till this time."- she said and took a deep breath in the memory of the past.

This is the same thing I also do or even feel about! whenever I think of her name "Ishana". I kept my silence for what all else she has to tell.

"One day, when Evelyn messaged me and told, how much you love me. I understood that how much value you are giving to me and how lucky I would be if I am yours's."- she said, with a lot of hope and love in her eyes.

She is wrong! That I will be the one who will be lucky if she is with me. Because all these what I have ever achieved and even my girlfriend "Eve" came into my life just because of her, in some way. I curiously looked at her while she was telling what all I ever wanted to hear from her.

"She just told me that she is your best friend but when I came here, I understood that how much she loves you and also watched the way you care for her."- by Saying this Ishana started getting very emotional again.

She puts me in pure silence and I can't even look into her eyes. I put my head down with a huge regret in my mind for losing her by a decision that I took in my life. The hardest thing is when we regret the most beautiful thing in your life. For me "Eve" is something irreplaceable and regretting it is like something worse.

Cutting my silence, she continued to express her feelings.

"I don't deserve you, otherwise she would have not come to your life. I know that I will miss you for sure but I just want to tell you that I love you too."- she said and burst into tears.

This was the word I ever wished to hear from her and maybe I can achieve the ultimate goal that I ever in my life but being selfish in my love would even kill the divinity that I put in the love for my Ishana. I know Evelyn would have even sacrifice her love for making us stay together because otherwise, she wouldn't have brought Ishana till here. But sacrificing her would be the greatest mistake that I could ever make"- All these thoughts gave me clarity in my mind.

Wiping all the tears apart and holding her hands to my heart I told Ishana "If we have another life in this world, I promise that I will be yours and, in this life, I am destined to love my 'Eve' and that I don't want to trade-off for anything in this world."

Without telling a single word she hugged me tight and kissed me on my forehead saying- "Do I at least deserve this, in this lifetime?" by putting a fake smile on her face.

It is really hard to see her smiling in this way and I am sure that I am never going to forget her and her place in my heart will be there forever but it's our decisions that determine our self-respect and integrity. I am a man with strong ethics and Evelyn has already given me her heart and soul. So, for me, Eve is like an unexpected gift in my life and I don't want to lose her for whatever reason. She gave me a second life and loved me as what I am and I was sure that she will hold my hand for sure if she was in my position.

"We will forget everything by itself, just give some time for yourself. like I would do."- by saying that, I hold her hand and take her out of my room.

Evelyn was sitting in the drawing-room waiting for us.

When she saw us, she stood up and comes near

me. Through her soda glass, I could see her eyes filled with tension and curiosity.

"Are you happy now! You got your dream girl, isn't it?"- she asked.

"Yes! Thank you so much for bringing her to me."- I said and give her a hug

Tears started flowing limitless from her eyes and she didn't even know what to tell next. Looks like she didn't expect a reply like this from me.

"Close your eyes, you have given me a surprise and I also want to give you one."- I said and I asked Ishana to close her eyes.

She was like in a mood of running away from there but what else she could do, when I am the one who is asking her to do it.

I take the ring from my pocket and I ask Ishana to take out the hands.

"Now open your eyes."- I told Evelyn.

At the moment she opened her eyes I kneeled on the floor and raised the ring towards her and asked "Will you marry me?".

I was hoping for a normal proposal but by bringing

Ishana to me she made it pretty dramatic by making me propose in front of my dream girl itself.

She broke out into tears again and jump into me like she always does, for that tight hug and while she stays close to my heart and my dream girl in front of my eyes. My mind said, "Evelyn is your girl, not in your dreams but your reality".

At that time, I understood the meaning of life and how all destiny could play in our lives. It was not about my dreams or my dream girl but about what all destiny could bring to you and how you are going to value it. Because you never know how valuable your life can offer you, over the dreams that you could ever dream of. In this life, I am not destined for Ishana that's also not because of my fate but because of my decision that I took for myself. You could say that I am a failure in my love but I am not running the race you are and I would like to say that I am a success in my love because I loved her and still, I love her and she also understood my love. So, what else anyone could ever achieve in their love to become a success. Sometimes it's not necessary to take our love to the next level but just being truthful is enough and even a sacrifice will not cause any harm to the divinity we have in that love. Also, it's not necessary to trade-off what you already have for a bigger dream because keep in your mind that even you are the one who put standards for your dream. Life doesn't end here and the story of Prajwal will continue and his dreams too.

MY MANTRA FOR A BEAUTIFUL LIFE

"Love deeply without expectations and leave them the choice to love you back or not."- **My heart.**

"Dreams may not be a thing that needs to be succeeded but it's a thing which can make us aspire to achieve many other goals in our life."- **My Consciousness.**

"It's not necessary to choose a hard time goal over a thing that gets you for easy because sometimes the easy thing can get you more happiness than the hardest thing."- **My Brain.**

"Don't believe what you see unless you have the full picture."- **My Eyes.**

"Don't open your ears to whatever you hear, leave the negatives even if it's helpful to you."- **My Ears.**

"Promises are free to give but hard to maintain. So, give it only if you have the guts to hold on."- **My Mouth.**

"Sacrificing what you had at the bad time for something at the good times may give you more happiness but kill your self-dignity."- **My Hands.**

"People will take you down for things you won't expect but, relying on your self-respect and ethics can make you the strongest weapon of positivity."- **My Attitude.**

"You may feel happy on cheating someone but, they are the ones who trust you whether it's your friend or your enemy."- **My Dignity.**

"Ethics are hard to maintain but, if you are strong enough to follow then not even God can decide the standards for your happiness."- **My Word.**

"Don't follow the principles of some random successful person, you are not here to race for some other life." **- My Life.**

ACKNOWLEDGEMENTS

I would like to express my gratitude to my life, my struggles, my pains, my sufferings, and my losses for making me what I am today and I would like to acknowledge My mother, who is the only role model in my life for being a strong pillar of love in my life for all the time irrespective of what I am and teaching me all the values of life through her, own life.

I want to thank my loving sister, other persons in my family, and all other beautiful people around who love me and support me.

After my mother, if there is someone in the place of it! They are my teachers. I want to thank all my teachers in my life irrespective of how much they love or care for me, I am expressing my huge gratitude from the bottom of my heart.

Finally, I would like to thank you for reading my book and sorry in advance if I disappoint you in any way because I can't determine the standards for you to like my work but I promise I will try my level best to give you something valuable as any true friend would do.

Send me your suggestions and feedback to: -

Facebook- : Durgadas BR
Instagram- : Durgadas_BR_Official
YouTube-   : DBR Talks
LinkedIn- : Durgadas BR
Twitter-   : Durgadas BR

9 789354 387050